A Book Of

MANAGEMENT CONTROL SYSTEM

For

BBA Semester - VI

As Per New Syllabus w.e.f. 2015

Dr. Pradip Kumar Sinha

M.Com, L.L.B.; A.C.A.; F.I.C.W.A.; A.C.I.S.(London), A.C.S., D.M.A. (ICA),Ph.D (Mgt)

Price ₹ 160.00

NIRALI PRAKASHAN
ADVANCEMENT OF KNOWLEDGE

N3464

Management Control System (BBA - VI)   **ISBN 978-93-5164-838-3**

Second Edition   :   **January 2017**

©   :   **Author**

Published By :

NIRALI PRAKASHAN

Abhyudaya Pragati, 1312, Shivaji Nagar
Off J.M. Road, PUNE – 411005
Tel - (020) 25512336/37/39, Fax - (020) 25511379
Email : niralipune@pragationline.com

➤ DISTRIBUTION CENTRES

PUNE

Nirali Prakashan : 119, Budhwar Peth, Jogeshwari Mandir Lane, Pune 411002, Maharashtra
Tel : (020) 2445 2044, 66022708, Fax : (020) 2445 1538
Email : bookorder@pragationline.com, niralilocal@pragationline.com

Nirali Prakashan : S. No. 28/27, Dhyari, Near Pari Company, Pune 411041
Tel : (020) 24690204 Fax : (020) 24690316
Email : dhyari@pragationline.com, bookorder@pragationline.com

MUMBAI

Nirali Prakashan : 385, S.V.P. Road, Rasdhara Co-op. Hsg. Society Ltd.,
Girgaum, Mumbai 400004, Maharashtra
Tel : (022) 2385 6339 / 2386 9976, Fax : (022) 2386 9976
Email : niralimumbai@pragationline.com

➤ DISTRIBUTION BRANCHES

JALGAON

Nirali Prakashan : 34, V. V. Golani Market, Navi Peth, Jalgaon 425001,
Maharashtra, Tel : (0257) 222 0395, Mob : 94234 91860

KOLHAPUR

Nirali Prakashan : New Mahadvar Road, Kedar Plaza, 1st Floor Opp. IDBI Bank
Kolhapur 416 012, Maharashtra. Mob : 9850046155

NAGPUR

Pratibha Book Distributors : Above Maratha Mandir, Shop No. 3, First Floor,
Rani Jhanshi Square, Sitabuldi, Nagpur 440012, Maharashtra
Tel : (0712) 254 7129

DELHI

Nirali Prakashan : 4593/21, Basement, Aggarwal Lane 15, Ansari Road, Daryaganj
Near Times of India Building, New Delhi 110002 Mob : 08505972553

BENGALURU

Pragati Book House : House No. 1, Sanjeevappa Lane, Avenue Road Cross,
Opp. Rice Church, Bengaluru – 560002.
Tel : (080) 64513344, 64513355,Mob : 9880582331, 9845021552
Email:bharatsavla@yahoo.com

CHENNAI

Pragati Books : 9/1, Montieth Road, Behind Taas Mahal, Egmore,
Chennai 600008 Tamil Nadu, Tel : (044) 6518 3535,
Mob : 94440 01782 / 98450 21552 / 98805 82331,
Email : bharatsavla@yahoo.com

niralipune@pragationline.com | www.pragationline.com

Also find us on 🅕 www.facebook.com/niralibooks

Preface ...

I am happy to present the book Management Control Systems for the students of management studies. The book provides comprehensive treatment of the theory and practice of Management Control norms and of the design of management control systems.

This book has been recognised and widely accepted by the students of Management studies and managers in the corporates who are involved or are affected by the Management control process. The book will be found useful by a wide section of readers, teachers and students of any stream and aspirants of business. The entire book is freshly written and thoroughly revised. The book has its own unique features. It brings out the subject in a very simple and lucid manner for easy and comprehensive understanding and the language used in this book is easy and simple to understand.

We would like to thank Mr. Jignesh Furia of Nirali Prakashan, and Ms. Supriya Singh, Mrs. Kumkum Tripathi for their constant support in completing this book, Akbar Shaikh, Ravindra Walodre and Chaitali Takle for typesetting, layout and art work and for visually enhancing the text.

Finally, I am grateful to my wife Shukla and children Pritish and Sanchari for their untiring support and patience without which the publication of this book was not possible.

Comments from the users would be welcome.

Author

●●●

Syllabus ...

1. Introduction to Management Control System

1.1 The Control Function: Elements of Control - Nature of Control - Problems in Control.

1.2 Management Control: Characteristics, Principles and Types of Management Control.

1.3 Factors affecting Managerial Philosophy.

1.4 Management Control Systems: Elements of MCS - Designing of MCS - 10 Commandments of Effective Control System.

2. Management Controls in Functional Areas

2.1 Production Control: Need - Procedure - Techniques of Production Control.

2.2 Inventory Control: Classification of Inventories - Motives for Holding Inventories - Determination of Stock Levels.

2.3 Marketing Control: Process of Marketing Control - Importance of Marketing Control System - Tools and Techniques of Marketing Control.

2.4 Control in Personnel Area: Reasons for Workers Resistance to Controls - Kind of Control Devices.

2.5 IT Measures and Control: Installation of Management Information and Control System, Structured and Unstructured Decision.

3. Computers Systems

3.1 Computer for Management Control Purposes - Are Computers essential for MIS?

3.2 Computers and Information System - Manual Systems - Mechanical Systems - MIS - Decision Support Systems - Characteristics of DSS - Where to apply DSS - Expert Systems.

4. Management Control of Projects

4.1 Meaning of project - Aspects of Project - Factors affecting Project.

4.2 Project Planning - Time Dimension - Cost Dimension-Quality Dimension.

4.3 Project Control - Reports Costs and Time- Reports on output Revisions.

5. Implementing MCS for Small and Medium Size Companies

5.1 Methodology of implementing Management Controls - Roles and Responsibilities in implementing Management Control.

5.2 Management Control Structure - Responsibility centre, cost centre, profit centre, investment centre.

5.3 MCS in service and non-profit organisations.

●●●

Contents ...

•••

Chapter **1**...

Introduction to
Management Control System

Contents ...

Learning Objectives ...

- To understand the elements and nature of control in organisations
- To explain the characteristics and types of management control
- To discuss the elements and designing of management control systems
- To highlight the ten commandments of effective control system
- To explain the factors affecting managerial philosophy

1.1 Control

1.1.1 Definition of Control

Control is seeing that the original performance is directed towards the expected performance. It is a significant function of management and is connected with all the other management functions. Control is a comparison and verification process and with the assistance of this process, a balance in the organisation activities that are directed towards the goals that are set can be attained and maintained. It helps in taking reformative measures in case it moves away from the planned course of action.

According to **Ernest Dale**, "The modern concepts of control envisages a system that only provides a historical record of what has happened to the business as a whole but pinpoints the reasons why it has happened and provides data that enable the chief executive or the departmental head to take corrective steps if he finds that he is on the wrong track."

According to **Koontz and O'Donnell**, "Controlling is the measurement and correction of the performance of activities of subordinates in order to make sure that enterprise objectives and the plans devised to attain them are being accomplished". Thus managerial function of control implies measurement of the original performance, comparing it with the standards set by plans and correction of deviations to guarantee achievement of goals in accordance with the plans.

According to **Henri Fayol**, the father of modern operational management theory, "Control consists in verifying whether everything occurs in conformity with the plans adopted, the instructions issued and principles established. It has an object to point out weaknesses and errors in order to rectify them and prevent recurrence. It operates on everything, things, people and their actions."

According to **George R. Terry**, "Controlling is determining what is being accomplished, that is, evaluating the performance and, if necessary, applying corrective measures so that the performance takes place according to plans".

Once a plan begins to function, control is needed to measure the progress, to reveal deviation from plans and to show and apply a correct action. The corrective action may even include a modification of plan, restructuring of the organisation, improving staffing and introducing changes in methods of guiding and leading.

Thus, controlling implies deciding and stating particularly what is to be achieved, then checking the performances against such standards that are recommended with the intention of giving the corrective action needed to attain the planned objectives. The end objective of controlling is, therefore, to guarantee that the people's efforts in the organisation are constantly directed towards the achievement of fixed goals.

To summarise, the meaning and purpose of control is:

1. Understanding exactly what work is to be completed as to (a) quantity; (b) quality; and (c) time available.

2. Understanding what resources are available for doing the work as to (a) personnel; (b) materials; and (c) other facilities.

3. Understanding that the work has been completed or is being completed (a) with the resources available; (b) within the time available; (c) at a reasonable cost; and (d) in keeping with the required standard of quality.

4. Knowing instantly of any setbacks, holdups or deviation as to (a) what happened; (b) its cause; and (c) solution.

5. Knowing what is being done and to get rid of such obstacles as to (a) who is doing; (b) how it is being completed; (c) what it is costing; and (d) when it will be done.

6. Knowing about the work that is finished as to (a) time ended; (b) quantity; and (c) final cost.

7. Knowing that resources are watched against (a) in what way; (b) by whom; (c) at what cost; and (d) with what provision for periodic check.

1.1.2 Introduction to Control Function

Control is an important function of management in every organisation. The management process is incomplete and at times ineffective without the control function. The management process consists of:

(i)   Planning
(ii) Organising
(iii) Staffing
(iv) Leading
(v)   Controlling

1. **Planning** pre-determines the objectives a manager intends to accomplish.

2. **Organising** provides the structure of an organisation by deciding how and where the employees will be positioned in the organisation and the responsibilities that they will require to complete to achieve predefined goals.

3. **Staffing** involves the managerial function of placing the right individual in the right job in the organisation.

4. **Leading** involves the managerial function of controlling, encouraging and directing the human resources of the organisation to attain organisational objectives.

5. The **control function** is concerned with guaranteeing that the planning, organising, staffing and leading functions result in the achievement of organisational goals. In other words, control is the tool that helps organisations in measuring and comparing their actual progress with their set plan.

Difference with Supervision

The word 'control' has different meanings in different contexts. In the management context, 'control' refers to the assessment of performance and the implementation of corrective actions to achieve organisational goals. Some individuals confuse the term 'control' with 'supervision.' Supervision is an element of control; it assists in identifying deviations from the set standards of performance.

Control as a Function

In order to see the managerial function of control in a correct viewpoint, it must be regarded taking into consideration the other functions of the manager. Control is one of the main functions of the manager at any level of a venture whether president or a foreman and in every project whether business, government, education or other type. These functions all of which are essential to the job of getting things completed through individuals and all of which vary from those of the engineer, accountant, mechanist, or personnel expert.

It is easily seen that all the functions of the manager are intimately inter-related. It is hard to determine when one function ends and another starts. Planning and controlling are particularly closely connected since the reason for control is to ensure that the plans are completed. Any effort taken to control without planning would be worthless since no one can tell whether his subordinates are doing what he needs them to do unless he first understands what his needs are. **Goetz** is of the opinion that "Management planning seeks consistent, integrated and articulated programs", while "Management control seeks to compel events to conform to plans." Plan thus forms the criteria for control.

1.1.3 Elements of Control: Process of Control

There are six elements of control, namely, authority, knowledge, guidance, direction, constraint and restraint. To be in a position to use control, the manager must understand what the situation is, what it should be, and how to correct it. In addition, he should have the power to take suitable action.

Control is an ongoing process which may be defined in terms of its sub-parts, as indicated and explained below.

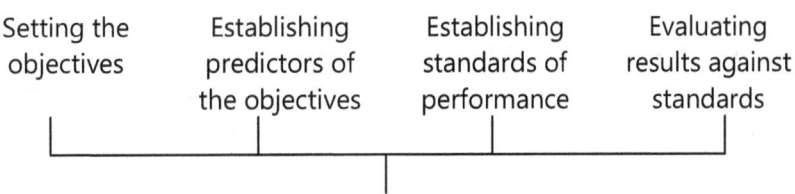

Feedback action to reinforce the positive and correct the negative results

Fig 1.1: Process of Control

(i) **Setting objectives:** Objectives must be established in measurable terms for the people plus the different work groups. This takes place during planning, if planning is completed well. By making clear what is desired of the enterprise and of the people and the groups within it, management by objectives serves as the connection between planning and control.

(ii) **Establishing predictors of the objectives:** Effective managers do not wait for a particular time to discover whether the objectives are being accomplished. They look for standard, dependable and punctual indicators. For example weekly or monthly sales results emphasising the problems by product/service and territory give managers a chance to help define and correct those problems. An effective flow of information and feedback system are important parts of a system for deciding whether the objectives are being attained or not.

(iii) **Establishing standard of performance:** As much as possible, each objective should indicate in detail the minimum standards of performance that are acceptable. These standards are based on past performance that is projected into the future and is established by managerial judgement or for some units developed through comprehensive studies for example, time studies for personal jobs.

(iv) **Evaluating results against standards:** When the manager sees the results early enough to take action on them, he or she decides which are important, which bear watching and which can be momentarily overlooked based on the amount of their deviation from standards and the importance of the items that are involved.

Thus, for example a 5 percent deficit in sales in the company's smallest territory on a minor good is not equivalent to a 30 percent loss on its biggest product in its biggest territory.

1.1.4 Nature of Control

Managerial control has the following features.

1. **Control process is cyclical:** The control process is cyclical which implies that it is never completed. Controlling leads to recognition of new problems that in turn requires to be addressed through setting up performance standards and measuring performance etc.

2. **Control is a function of management:** It is actually a follow-up action to the other functions of management; this function is carried out by all the managers in the organisation to control the activities that are allotted to them.

3. **Control is a dynamic process:** It involves a constant review of standards of performance and results in corrective action which may cause a change in other functions of management.

4. **Employees often view controlling negatively:** By its very nature, controlling frequently causes a change in behaviour that is expected by the management. Despite how positive the changes may be for the organisation, the employees may still look at them negatively.

5. **Control is both anticipatory and retrospective:** The process expects problems and takes anticipatory action. With corrective action, the process also follows up on problems.

1.1.5 Importance of Control

The importance of control in management is as follows:

1. **Reduces risk:** Control removes the risk of non-conformity of the original performance with the major goals of the organisation. Control is the function which controls the operation to guarantee the achievement of the set objectives.

   Regular measurement of work in progress with proper adjustments in operations puts the performance on the right track and helps in achieving goals.

2. **Basis for future action:** Control gives the information and facts to the management for planning and organising when the work is finished and the result is assessed. In fact, assessment of results assists the management re-plan for non-repetitive operations and satisfying, punishing and disciplining the employees.

   It is better to say that the future long-term planning is impossible unless and until control information is accessible in time for the managers to operate their work.

3. **Size of the business:** In big scale business in the modem times it is not possible to work without appropriate policies, procedures and quality of different varieties of products. That is why in a big scale organisation there is always a requirement of a scientific system of control to solve the daily problems.

4. **Indicator for managerial weakness:** In the organisation there is a certain unexpected and unknown problem which cannot be marked out by mere planning, organising and staffing efforts. It is the control process that can mark these out. That is why it is called as a pointer of the managerial weakness. Control not only discovers the weakness of managers but also gives solutions and remedial action to solve the problems.

5. **Facility of co-ordination:** Management and co-ordination of the business activities and employees is a very significant role. It binds all the employees and their activities and encourages them to approach the common objectives through co-ordination.

   Control plays the role of a middleman between the employees and management to give the necessary data in time to the employees.

6. **Simplifies supervision:** An efficient system of control assists in finding out the deviation that exists in the organisation which also makes the task easy for the supervisor in managing his subordinates. So through control it becomes easier for the supervisor to manage and direct the employees to pursue the right track and complete the necessary goals.

7. **Extension of decentralisation:** Control system assists the top management in expanding the borders of decentralisation without the loss of control. When the correct procedures, policies, targets, etc. are clearly expressed to the subordinates, they develop self-confidence and do not always consult their supervisors with the problems.

1.1.6 Types of Control

According to the systems approach every open system processes inputs from the surrounding environment to generate a unique set of outputs. The human body is a natural open structure which preserves a life-sustaining balance through regular feedback mechanisms like shivering or perspiring. Then again, man-made open systems like the organisation do not have such automatic control mechanisms. They need continuous observation and control to avoid deviations from standards. Controls can be used before an activity begins (feed forward control), while the activity is taking place (concurrent control), or after the activity has been finished (feedback). Fig. 1.2 show three types of controls.

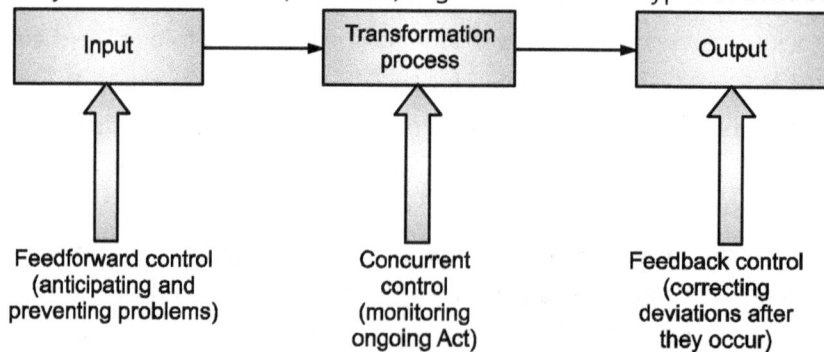

Fig. 1.2: Types of Control

1. Feedforward control

Feed forward control is introducing anticipated problems. As the name proposes, as it occurs before the actual activity, it is future-directed. Though feedback control is connected to planning, the two have different procedures. Planning answers the question, "Where are we leaving?" while feedforward control addresses itself to the question, "What can we do ahead of time to help our plan to be successful?" Employing workers prior to the implementation of a diversification plan stops possible delays.

Feedforward control is like preventive maintenance. For example, the Airlines are required to carry out a preventive feedforward and control for all its aircraft so as to become aware of and prevent structural damage than cause tragic situations. Feedforward control is significant because it stops problems from happening. This kind of control is possible and effective only when correct information is available on time.

2. **Concurrent control**

Concurrent control or real-time control occurs while altering activities are in progress. For instance, while reserving your seat in a computerised railway booking office, the booking clerk uses concurrent control so that he does not make a mistake of assigning seats to the passengers at the same time. Modern production technology is created to give operators an instant response if any mistake is made. If you input the wrong command, the program's concurrent controls decline your command and might tell you why it is not right.

3. **Feedback control**

This is the most famous type of control. Feedback control takes place, after an activity has taken place. The manger collects data about an activity that is finished, assesses that information and takes steps to develop similar activities in the future. For example, by checking the complaints obtained from the students about billing, a hostel's hall manager finds out that the performance of his mess clerk needs attention. Because corrective action is taken to change the fact, costs have a tendency to increase quickly and problems and differences persist.

Feedback control has many benefits over feedforward and concurrent control. Firstly, it gives information on the efficiency of its planning effort. The greater the difference between standard and actual performance the manager can use this data for establishing future plans. Secondly, it gives information to the employee on how well they are doing. It thus behaves like a motivator.

The major control types based on timing are discussed below.

Stages of Production		Type of Control	Description
Input	Capital	Feedforward	Inputs are monitored to ensure that they meet the standards necessary for the transformation process.
	Labour		
	Raw Materials		
	Market Information		
	Equipment		

contd. ...

Transformation Process	Planning	Concurrent	Regulates ongoing activities that are a part of the transformation process to ensure that they conform to organisational standards.
	Organising		
	Staffing		
	Leading		
	Controlling		
Output	Goods	Feedback	Exercised after a product or service has been produced to ensure that the final output meets quality standards and goals.
	Services		
	Profits		
	Waste Materials		

1.1.7 Problems of Control

1. **Excessive control:** The control mechanism is important for the organisation to function properly. Particularly, it guarantees effective supervision of employees, maintenance of quality, presence of suitable safety dimensions and observance of various technical processes. On the other hand, using too much control over employee behaviour can surely be damaging as they may feel anxious. Excessive control may make the employees work more out of fear, than out of enthusiasm to contribute.

2. **Perceived bias:** When employees believe that the control mechanism does not have objectivity in the fixation of standards, measures and rewards, they will probably oppose such control measures. In the same way, when the employees sense that the rewards are grossly inadequate for their performance, they may refuse to accept control initiatives.

3. **Tendency to avoid accountability:** Control needs employees to accept responsibility for their work activities. In truth, employees often make an error of linking responsibility with discipline and punishment. As a result, they try to control to avoid accepting any responsibility. The resistance can be harsher if the managers are not ensuring that the employees know about the goals and expectations clearly and also what is expected of them.

4. **Absence of employees' participation in the control process:** When employees are not engaged in the controlling process, they may feel alienated from it. They may also believe that all the control measures are forced on them externally. In such circumstances, they may refuse to accept the managers' efforts to establish a control system.

5. **Inconsistent focus:** When there are inherent disagreements in the goals, purposes or focus of the controlling function, employees may resist control if such disagreements will have any negative effect on the organisation or the person. For example, sales target that compels a sales person to follow high pressure tactics to accomplish short-term sales target that might generate a negative impact on the public image of the organisation in the long run.

1.2 Management Control

1.2.1 Introduction

Management control is the process of ensuring that resources are obtained, used effectively and efficiently in achieving the organisation's objectives. Management control process is carried on within the framework established by strategic planning. The objectives, facilities, organisation and financial factors are more or less established as given. For example, decisions taken about next year's budget. The reason for management control system is to motivate the managers to act in the best interests of the firm.

Management control can be defined as a systematic effort by business management to compare performance to set standards, plans or objectives so as to decide whether the performance is along the lines of these standards and most probably with the intention of taking any corrective action that is required to see that the business and other corporate resources are being used in the most efficient way possible in obtaining corporate objectives.

All control begins with a company's plans and expectations for the future, that is, goals and standards against which performance is calculated. In an operational control condition, a means of obtaining correct and new data about the existing performance should be developed next. The original is then compared with the expected; when there is any deviation from the standard, some kind of action is taken.

1.2.2 Characteristics of Effective Control System

1. **Suitable:** The control system should suit the nature and requirements of the activity. The controls that are used in the sales department are different from those used in finance and for the workforce. In the same way, a machine-based technique of production needs a control system which is not as same as the system that is used in labour intensive techniques of production. Thus, every concern should develop such a control system that would serve its particular needs.

2. **Time and forward looking:** Even though it is an ideal control system, certain electric controls, should be capable of detecting deviations before they happen. Very similarly, this is not possible in personnel and marketing controls which always consist of a time interval between the deviation and remedial action. Regardless, the feedback system should be as small as possible and the information should reach the superior before it is too late to stop failures.

3. **Objective and comprehensible:** The control system should be both objective and clear. Objective controls state the expected results in clear and definite words and leave little room for argument by the workers. They stay away from red tape and give employees direct entry to any extra data which they may require to do their job. Employees are not made to go up and down the hierarchy to get the information. When the exact reason, for which the control system survives, is not understood, it is hard if not impossible to set up criteria for its assessment and review.

4. **Flexible:** The control system should be flexible so that it can be altered to suit the requirements of any change in the basic nature of the inputs and/or the sizes, varieties of types of a similar product or service. One way to introduce flexibility into a control system is to create adjustments that are automatic. Both flexible budgets and standard costs, for example, provide a changing standard for costs, as the quantity of work goes up or down. A same kind of adjustment is in operation when the sales quotas are tied to a business activity. In all such plans, the basis of changing the control standard is built right into the system.

5. **Economical:** Economy is another requirement of every control system. The profit that is derived from a control system should be more than the cost involved in applying it. To spend a rupee to protect 99 paisa is not control. It is a waste, that eighty years ago, was plainly understood by the people who built Sears, Roebuck and Company, the world's largest retail store. In the beginning of the main-order business, the money in incoming orders was not calculated. The orders were weighted and unopened. Sears, Roebuck and Company had run sufficient tests to understand what average weights correspond to overall amounts of money.

6. **Prescriptive and operational:** In order for a control system to be successful and sufficient it should not only detect deviations from the standards but should also give remedies to the problems that lead to deviations. In other words, the system should be prescriptive and operational. It must reveal where failures are happening, who is accountable for them and what should be done about them. It must concentrate more on action than on the data.

7. **Acceptable to organisation members:** The system should be acceptable to the organisation members. When standards are set independently by the upper level managers, there is a threat that employees will consider those standards as irrational or impractical. They may then decline to meet them. Status differences between people also have to be identified. The people, who have to report deviations to someone they make out to be a lower level staff member may stop taking the control system sincerely.

8. **Reveal exceptions of strategic points:** A control system should be such as to disclose exceptions at strategic points. Small exceptions in particular parts have larger importance than larger deviations in other parts. A five percent deviation from the standard in office labour cost is more significant than 20 percent deviation from the standard in cost of postage stamps. That we can measure something is no cause for measuring it. The question is, "Is this something a manager's attention should be concentrated on?"

1.2.3 Management Control Principles

The basic principles of management control can be divided into three categories reflecting their reason and nature, structure and process. These principles of management control are given below.

1. **Principle of Assurance of Objective:** The basic purpose of management control is the achievement of objectives by detecting any failures in plans. Prospective or definite deviations from plans should be identified as much as necessary to allow effective remedial action.

2. **Principle of Efficiency of Controls:** A management control system should detect and emphasise the causes of deviations from plans with least amount of costs and unnecessary results. The principle of efficiency is mainly significant in control because methods have a tendency to become costly and troublesome. A manager may be so involved in control that he spends more than it is necessary to detect a deviation. Controls which seriously interfere with authority of subordinates or self-esteem of those who implement plans, is ineffective.

3. **Principle of Control Responsibility:** The main responsibility for the exercise of control lies with the manager who is responsible for the implementation of plans. His responsibility cannot be ignored without altering the organisation structure. This easy principle clears the misunderstood role of the controllers and control units. These, agencies perform in a service or staffs give control information. But they cannot use control unless they are given the managerial power and responsibility to get the things under control.

4. **Principle of Forward Looking:** Control, like planning should be forward looking. The principle is frequently ignored mostly because control relies on accounting and statistical information instead on predictions and projections. Even though predictions are not precise, they are superior to historical records. Ideally, a control system should give an immediate feedback so that deviations from the desired performance are checked as soon as they happen. If this is not possible, control should be based on predictions, so as to foresee deviations eventually. For example, cash forecasts help in maintaining the solvency of business by anticipating cash shortages and avoiding them.

5. **Principle of Direct Control:** Most controls used today are based on the fact that human beings make errors. They are frequently used as indirect controls aimed at catching faults, regularly after the fact is stated. Wherever possible, direct controls intended to avoid mistakes should be used. Improving the quality of managers can decrease the need for indirect controls. High quality managers make very little mistakes and perform all their functions to the best advantage.

6. **Principle of Reflection of Plans:** Controlling is the task of making sure that plans are carried out effectively. Therefore, control techniques must reflect the specific nature and structure of plans. For example, cost control, must be based on planned costs of a definite and specific type.

7. **Principle of Organisational Suitability:** A management control system fits the authority area and reflects the organisation structure. When the management control system is customised to the structure of the organisation, it identifies the responsibility for action and facilitates correction of deviation from the plans. In the same way, the information to assess performance against plans must suit the position of the manager who is to use it. In other words, all figures and reports used for control should be in terms of the organisation.

8. **Principle of Individuality of Controls:** Controls become efficient when they are in agreement with the position, operational responsibility, competence, and requirements of the person concerned. The scope and detailed information required differ with the level and function of management. In the same way, different managers prefer different types and units of information that is to be reported. Therefore, controls should meet the personal needs of each manager.

9. **Principle of Critical Point Controls:** While implementing control, a manager should concentrate on the factors that are important for assessing a performance. It would be pointless and uneconomical for a manager to verify each and every detail of performance. Therefore, he should focus his attention only on the important points of performance.

10. **Principle of Action:** Control is a lost cause unless the corrective action is taken. Corrective action involves redrawing of plans, reorganisation, substitution or training of a subordinate, encouraging staff members, etc. Control is warranted only when deviations that are shown from plans are corrected through suitable planning, organising, staffing and directing.

1.2.4 Types of Management Control

Control systems in an organisation fall under two wide areas: formal and informal.

Formal controls are given in writing by the management, whereas informal controls come up as a consequence of employees' behaviour. Examples of formal controls are plans, budgets, regulations and quotas. Informal controls consist of group customs and organisational culture. Formal controls are outlined by the managers, whereas informal controls frequently start off with employees and are affected by general socio-cultural factors.

(A) Formal Control System

Formal control systems are written, management-initiated mechanisms that control the behaviour of employees in attaining the organisation's goals. Formal controls can be divided into three types on the basis of the nature of management intervention that are as follows.

1. **Input controls:** These are the actions that are taken by the firm before a planned activity is executed. These measures assist the firm in choosing the right way to carry out the activity. Input controls consist of selection criteria, recruitment and training programs, manpower allotments, strategic plans and resource allocations. Process controls involve tracking particular variables and taking a correct action whenever there is any deviation from the specified limits in the variables. The control action happens before the process of change is finished and the output is generated. Process control is used when the company tries to control the ongoing activity to attain the required ends. The control is applied to the behaviour or activities instead of the end results. For example, under a feedforward system of inventory control, the factors that have an effect on inventory levels of completed goods, such as the rate of sales or dispatch delays, are followed. When the sales start reducing or there is a dispatch bottleneck, this information is fed forward, and the level of the finished goods inventory is controlled by reducing production. Thus, the inventory levels are stopped from going beyond the required levels. On the other hand, the managers may realise that the actual standards for sales or dispatch delays are no longer suitable and therefore should be altered. This again feeds into a loop, which later on updates the inventory objectives or plans. Process control can also be demonstrated using the example of a salesperson's job. The management may direct the salesperson to follow certain methods for new market development, but may not hold the salesperson accountable for the extent of new business created, that is, the end result. In such a case, process control has been used.

2. **Output controls:** Output control is used when performance standards are fixed and checked, and the results are assessed. Output control occurs when the control activity is based on the comparison of the original and planned results. Such controls are applicable when it is simple and economical to measure the output and when there are a small number of parts of uncertainty. In this kind of control, the management expects the employee to perform in a result-oriented way, as it believes that the employee has the necessary knowledge to carry out the activities that are required in an appropriate way, and to finish the task that is allotted without the management's interference.

(B) Informal Control System

These are unwritten, normally worker-initiated mechanisms that control the behaviour of the people or groups in business units. There are three types of informal controls. They are:

1. **Self-control:** It deals with the establishment of the individual goals by the person, monitoring their achievement and changing the behaviour in the organisation to achieve the goals. Self-control can be advantageous to an organisation if the organisation's goals are in accord with the person's objectives. But if the objectives do not match then the performance of the employee will suffer.

2. **Social control:** Social control refers to the current social viewpoints and patterns of interpersonal communication within subgroups in the company. In this type of control, an organisation sets certain standards, observes and checks conformity with the standard and takes action when deviations take place. Social control comes out of the internalisation of values and joint commitment towards some common objectives.

3. **Cultural control:** According to **William G. Ouchi**, culture is "the broader values and normative patterns that guide worker behaviour within the entire organisation." Cultural control can be realised by customs of social communication, and stories, rituals and tales that are connected to the organisation.

1.3 Management Control Systems

1.3.1 Introduction

A control system is a set of formal and informal systems to help the management in guiding the organisation towards its goals. A Management Control System (MCS) is a set of inter-related communication structures that ease the processing of data to help managers to co-ordinate the parts and achieve the purpose of the organisation on a constant basis. Therefore, management control system is a multidisciplinary topic as it requires contributions from all the branches that are related to management in attaining a high level of quality, productivity and innovation.

The word 'management control' has been defined in a different way by different authorities on the topic. According to **Anthony**, **Dearden** and **Govindarajan**, strategic planning, management control and task control are the three processes that are inter-related with planning and control. **William Newman** considers control an important part of the management process. **Katz**, **Kahn** and **Griesinger** see the whole organisation as a control system. **Maciariello** and **Kirby** say that the control of strategy and operations is a part of management control.

According to **Horngren,** "Management Control System is an incorporated method for gathering and using information to encourage employee behaviour and to assess the performance".

According to **Simons,** "Management Control Systems are the formal, information-based customs and processes managers use to maintain or change patterns in organisational activities".

According to **Maciariello**, "Management Control is related to co-ordination, resource allocation, motivation, and performance measurement. All organisations use both formal and informal control systems".

1.3.2 Elements of Management Control System

Every control system has at least four elements.

1. A **detector** or sensor, that is, a device that calculates what is really happening in the situation being controlled.
2. An **assessor**, that is, a device for deciding the importance of what is occurring, that is, comparison with some standard or expectation.
3. An **effector**, that is, a device that changes behaviour if the evaluator specifies the need. This device is frequently called as "feedback."
4. A **communication network**, that is, devices that transmit data between the detector and the evaluator and between the evaluator and the effector.

These four basic elements of any control system are shown in Fig. 1.3.

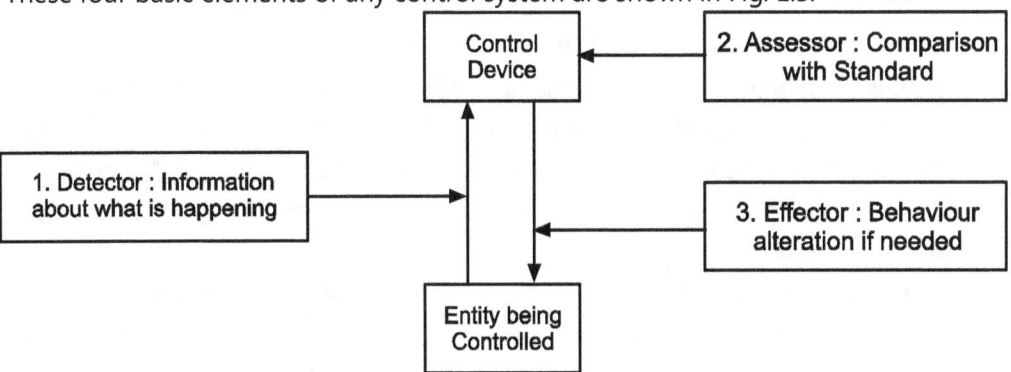

Fig. 1.3: Elements of Control Process

Moreover, consider a situation of an automobile driver on a highway where the speed limit is 65 kmph. The control system in this case acts as follows.

1. The eye (sensors) calculates the original speed by observing the speedometer.
2. The brain (assessor) compares the original speed with the desired speed upon detecting a deviation from the standard.

3. Directs the foot (effector) to facilitate or press down on the accelerator.

4. The nerves from the communication system that transmits data from the eyes to the brain and from the brain to the foot.

It would be seen that regulation of a car is difficult as there is no assurance as to what action the brain will guide after obtaining and assessing the information from the detector. For example, once the driver decides to keep the speed limit not exceeding 65 km per hour, some drivers who want to stay within the legal limit will relax, on the other hand others, for numerous reasons will not. In these circumstances, control is not automatic, one would have to understand something about the personality and conditions of the driver to forecast what the original speed of the automobile would be at the end point of the process.

The Management Control Process is more complex than what has been explained in detectors, evaluators, effectors and a communication system. These are as follows.

1. The standard is not predetermined. It is somewhat a result of conscious planning process where management makes a decision on what the organisation should be doing and as part of control process it is also compares the original with these plans.

2. Like controlling an automobile, management control is not automatic. Some of the detectors are mechanical, but the significant data is detected through the managers' own eyes, ears and other senses. The actions taken to alter the organisations behaviour involve people.

3. Unlike controlling a vehicle, management control requires co-ordination among the people. An organisation includes many separate parts and management control must make sure that each part synchronises with the others.

4. The relationship from perceiving the need for action and the action that is needed to obtain the desired result may not be comprehensible. In the function, as an evaluator the manager may come to a decision that the "costs are too high" but there is no simple or automatic action or a series of action that will bring the prices down to what the standards say.

5. Control in an organisation does not occur only as a result of actions. Much of the control is self-control that is, individuals act in the way they do, not mainly because they are given certain instructions by their boss, rather their own judgment tells them what action is suitable.

1.3.3 Designing of the Management Control System

There are certain steps of designing MCS in an organisation. They are as follows:

1. **Identification of Role of Employees:** The role of each employee right from the chief executive to the lowest rank employee is needed to be identified.

2. **Identification of Key Actions:** A correct identification of the required actions is crucial because the reason for MCS is to influence and control the actions of the employees. Thus, identification of actions that are important is necessary though they vary from organisation to organisation as well as level to level of organisation in which the employees carry out their tasks.

3. **Understanding of Role Demands and KRAs:** Role demands are required to be recognised from the Key Result Areas (KRAs). KRAs are the areas of growth for an organisation and they change as per the current climate of an internal as well as an external organisation.

4. **Understanding Likely Results of Role Demands:** The next step is to know about the likely results of the role demands. We can say that an organisation has succeeded in applying MCS when it is observed that there is no dissimilarity between the required action and the likely action. In case there is any difference between the two, the causes of difference have to be discovered and reported for taking a correct action.

5. **Choice of Controls:** Control mechanisms are chosen from different options. A specific control mechanism can be chosen based on the level and depth of the problem. On the whole, two types of controls are accepted by the management of an organisation; the types of controls are action controls and result controls.

   Action control is the way for achieving work efficiency; they work on procedures that are established and are directly connected to the tasks that are to be performed; they can be accepted evenly and in a co-ordinated manner all through the organisation. On the other hand, these controls do not motivate creativity and innovation among the employees since these controls are inflexible and are used for everyday jobs.

6. **Result Controls are Used to Control the Employees' Behaviour:** That is why these controls are also called as behavioural controls. By using these controls the managers inform the employees about what they are supposed to do so as to generate the desired results. So, the managers' state, the dimensions and areas of work on which controls will be used by way of measuring the original performances against the set standards and offering enough incentives to motivate employees to perform well. In truth, these controls increase motivation and improve commitments among employees to perform their jobs effectively. On the other hand, any problem arising out of these controls is usually credited to the mistakes made by the employees.

7. **Use of Mixed Controls:** The controls can be used by the management firmly or loosely. The managers should be cautious in exercising the extent of tightness or looseness of controls, which depend on how the organisation understands the issues like, the benefits of exercising tight or loose controls, cost incurred in exercising

controls, side-effects of tight or loose controls, etc. Therefore, the best advantage can be attained by an organisation if it uses mixed controls, that is, a combination of tight and loose controls, by which the benefits of both types of controls in terms of creativity, innovation and also inflexibility can be accomplished by the management.

1.3.4 Ten Commandments of Effective Control System

The following are ten important or basic needs of an effective control system.

1. **Suitable:** The control system should be appropriate for the type of activity that is meant to be served. Apart from differences in the systems of control in different business, they also differ from department to department and from one level in the organisation to the other. A system of control helpful at a higher level of management will be hard in the extent and nature from that in use at the operative level. Many methods are available for control reasons such as budgets, break-even points, financial ratios and so on. The manager should be certain that he is using the method that is suitable for control of the particular activity that is involved. The tool that is suitable is not necessarily equivalent between different departments or between two different establishments. For instance, the sales department and production department may use different tools of control. Again, a small business will not have a control system as detailed as a big organisation.

2. **Understandable:** The system must be understandable, that is, the control information that is given should be understood by those who use it. A control system that a manager cannot understand is bound to remain unproductive. The control information given should be such as will be used by the managers concerned. What is considered important and understandable to one manager may not be so to another. It is, thus, the responsibility of the manager concerned to ensure that the control information that is given to him is of a nature that will be useful. As an illustration, it is likely that top managers may understand a difficult system of control based on numerical break-even charts and mathematical formulae whereas to the lower level manager such data would be of little use, being beyond their powers of understanding. In this sense, the data that is given as information should be understandable and helpful.

3. **Economical:** The system must be reasonable in process, that is, the cost of a control system while it is being used should not go beyond the possible savings. The extent of control required must be decided by the standard of precision or quality needed. A very high degree or standard of accuracy or quality may not really be required. Unwarranted difficulty of the control system should be avoided to keep a check on the costs of control. It, thus, becomes essential to focus the control system on factors, which are strategic to keep the costs down and the system inexpensive.

4. **Flexible:** The system of control should be flexible even if the plans have to be altered. In case the control systems can work only because of one particular plan, it becomes ineffective if the plan fails and another has to be replaced. However carefully the plans may have been made or the planning premises established, unexpected situations can disturb the best-laid plans. A good control/system would be adequately flexible to allow the changes so necessitated. For example, **Goetz** indicated that it was possible that some particulars within the plan might go down. The control system must report about such failures and should have adequate elements or flexibility to maintain a managerial control of functions despite such failures.

5. **Expeditious:** Nothing can be done to correct deviations, which have already taken place. It is, thus, significant that the control system should report deviations from plans that are expeditious. A deviation that is detected months after it takes place serves no useful purpose. The aim of the control system should be to correct deviations in the immediate future. This requires that the time-lag between the event of a deviation and its reporting be kept at the minimum possible.

6. **Forward Looking:** The control system should thus look forward as the manager cannot control the past. In fact, the control system can sometimes be so planned as to expect possible deviations or problems. Thus, deviations can be predicted so that corrections can be included even before the problem takes place. Cash forecasts and cash control is an example in point where a financial manager can predict the future cash needs and provide for them beforehand.

7. **Organisational Conformity:** Since people perform various activities and events must be controlled through individuals, it is important that the control data and system must obey the organisational pattern. The control data must be well prepared so that it is possible to fix accountability for the deviations within the areas of responsibility. For example, where factory costs are gathered in a way other than on the basis of areas of responsibility, they may lose much of their importance as a tool of control. In this case, the original costs in a department may be unequal to the standards set without the department knowing whether the deviation has been caused by something within its control. In this sense, organisation and control are hard to separate, where they are reliant on one another for effective management.

8. **Indicative of Exception at Critical Points:** The management principle of exception should be used to show up not only deviations but the important areas must also be fixed for effective control.

9. **Objectivity:** As far as possible measurements must be used, particularly while assessing a subordinate's performance, the subjective element cannot be completely

eliminated. Here the personality of both the manager as well as his subordinate would be reflected in the final judgement and bias the evaluation. These indefinite words can irritate the subordinate like being told that he is not doing a fine job. He will probably react more positively towards objective standards.

10. **Suggestive of Corrective Action:** In the end, a sufficient control system should not only detect failures but also reveal where they are taking place, whether it is accountable for them and what should be done to correct them. Overall summary information can conceal particular fault areas. For example, it is not enough to show only a decline in the profits. The reason for such decline, such drop in the sales volume or an increase in the costs can also be shown. Even this is not enough. The information should also reveal in which market areas the sales declined and specific costs have increased. Where a system just detects deviations but does not show any corrective action, the control system becomes futile.

1.3.5 Factors Influencing the Design of Management Control System

The design of control systems is controlled by numerous factors: managerial style, corporate culture, organisation structure, organisational slack, stakeholders' control and communication structures. Management style and corporate culture play a significant role in designing the control system. The management style is connected to the individual manager whereas corporate culture relates to the overall organisational idea. In fact management style and corporate culture are related to one another. A manager's style influences other managers' sense of fashion in the organisation and on the culture of an organisation. Culture includes shared values and customs of the organisation and this influences the style that exists in the management. Hence, management style and culture are linked.

1. **Managerial Styles and the Design of Control Systems**

Managers vary in their styles of managing employees. The different styles have an effect on the design of the control systems. If the control systems are not designed with the managerial style in mind, then conflicts might occur between organisational objectives and managerial styles. The different managerial styles that influence the design of control systems are external control, internal control and mixed control.

(a) **External control:** External control works on the idea that subordinates can be encouraged through rewards. This style is commanding and mechanical as the organisational objectives are established by the top management.

(b) **Internal control:** This style works on the idea that subordinates will be encouraged and remain loyal to the organisation if they are involved in the decision-making process. The style supposes that employees will experience a sense of accomplishment, recognition and self-esteem if they are involved in the decision-making process.

(c) **Mixed control:** The two types of control that were discussed above have their own benefits and drawbacks. Hence a manager has to cautiously analyse the advantage of each style and carefully selects the style that would be most advantageous to the organisation.

2. Corporate Culture and Design of Control Systems

Corporate culture assists in co-ordinating all the activities of an organisation. In an organisation when the objectives and values are shared by the individual members, problems are reduced and a sense of group loyalty prevails. For example, IBM has designed the following belief system for its employees.

(a) Respect for the individual.

(b) Customer service.

(c) Dedication to work towards excellence.

(d) Decentralised business.

(e) Total quality management.

(f) Empowerment of people.

Employees should also be rewarded suitably for understanding and executing the ideas recommended by the management and attaining new goals. At times, due to resistance from the leader certain changes are prevented from being executed. In such cases, it is better to change the leader. After the change has been implemented, it is significant to expand it to other sub-systems of the control system.

3. Decentralisation and Design of Control Systems

It is essential for every organisation to decentralise the decision-making authority, so that sub-goals can be established. Like this, every decision-maker is made accountable only for a small part of the overall organisational goal. Decentralisation guarantees that the decision-maker arrives at the right decision by making use of adequate information. On the other hand, decision-makers should find ways to cope with the difficulty in the organisational environment even when the information available to them is inadequate. The reason for a control system is to join the sub-units of an organisation together. Without a centralised control system, it would be difficult to bring this about. What is significant for an organisation is not whether it should be decentralised or not, but to what length it should be decentralised.

4. Organisational Slack and Design of Control Systems

Richard M. Cyert and James G. March defines organisational slack as "the disparity between the resources available to the organisation and the payments required to maintain the coalition." Organisational slack happens when an organisation exploits its environment.

This exploitation results in higher salaries, wages and privileges that are required to complete the objectives of the company. Dividends may be higher than is needed to maintain the confidence of shareholders. But, in terms of management control systems, slack behaves like a cushion against changing the business environment and provides resources for innovation and adaptation in different areas.

5. Stakeholder Controls and Design of Control Systems

The stakeholders of an organisation consist of investors, customers, employees, suppliers and the public. It is important for the organisation to decide the objectives and performance measures of each of the categories that are mentioned above. A functional organisational structure is designed keeping these goals in view and then managerial controls are designed for departments of the organisation. Based on the associations and the objectives, organisations use control over stakeholders. The analysis of stakeholder associations starts with recognising all the stakeholders. The next step is to differentiate the significant stakeholders. This group includes stakeholders who are very important, powerful in as much as the organisation's decision-making process is concerned.

The next step is the analysis of the incentives that can be given to the stakeholders. Incentives consist of material rewards, power, distinction and taking part in the activities of the organisation. After that, the contribution for a specific stakeholder has to be analysed. Contributions consist of capital, revenue, performance and community support. Ultimately, the competition for a specific stakeholder is analysed. All these steps help the firm in recognising important stakeholder variables that assist in checking and influencing the control process.

6. Communication Structures and Control Process

The formal and informal communication within an organisation consist of meetings, day-to-day contacts among managers, body language etc. All these formal and informal communications are important in understanding and improving the control process. Let us talk about how communication structures support control process with the assistance of information systems. The first part of the information system is a formal or informal process, which examines the environment in which an organisational sub-unit works. After this the organisation needs a planning process. The planning stage is the most important of all, as it involves four sub-processes namely strategic planning, business planning, long range planning and operations planning. All these processes would remain unfinished without appropriate communication across different levels of the organisational hierarchy. Feedback is required after each stage is completed. The feedback is accumulated in the form of a report. This is followed by decision-making procedures and applying them.

1.4 Factors affecting Managerial Philosophy

Application of the concept of management control needs the following.

1. Recognising important factors in the business operation which need to be controlled so as to attain a given overall result;

2. Specifying the basis for establishing standards of performance for each control factor, such as forecasts, budgets, standard costs, turnover ratios and lead times;

3. Defining the information-accounting and operating data and statistics that must be collected to measure status and performance;

4. Establishing a reporting structure that recognises the performance in each control area, relates causes and effects, signals, trends, and recognises the results by responsibility under the plan of organisations.

The development of such a management control system needs a careful study of the total enterprise and its division into controllable parts. A close inspection must also be made of each part in terms of its operational features.

Four extra factors which operate to affect the managerial philosophy are –

1. **Measuring Business Data interferes with the Data Measured:** In business, as in several other areas of the social sciences, many a times the act of measuring gets in the way with the data being measured. The simple fact that an article (such as return on investment, inventory turnover or sales revenue) has been chosen for measurement attaches an unwanted bias and lack of objectivity of the item.

   Actions may be taken which are unreasonable in overall company terms in order to 'window dress' the item that is being measured. Executives who have worked under budgetary control may overstress the need to stay within the budget, often a loose sight of what should be their objective: economical and profitable operations. Situations that change very well justify deviation from the original budget, but even then, only an experienced executive freely discards the carefully prepared budget target.

2. **Measures of Business Data must be Appropriate:** An important requirement in management is to raise the ability to understand the important items in a given circumstance and to direct attention to them for correct identification of the problem and the parts that are important frequently provide the solution to the problem. Information which would concentrate its attention only on important events and results would give any manager much more and would result in much better performance than we have any right to expect under normal reporting systems.

3. **Diminishing Returns on Internal Management Controls:** The information and measurements in our control systems are easier to adapt to internal rather than external checking but the greatest opportunities lie outside the company. One feature of the control system should be assessment of outside income possibilities. Diversification and merger studies have made considerable improvements in recent years, yet the external aspects of control have been hardly explored by most firms. The whole field of private enterprise offers an opportunity for control system application.

4. **Business is a Unique Situation:** Business presents a unique form to those interested in controls and in control. Unlike all natural and mechanically working systems, it assesses an extensive variety of events and results that are of great importance to its successful operation, but which cannot simply be quantified within the current system of measurement.

Approached with a correct requisition for ultimate control which lies in decisions by 'individuals harmoniously at work' at all levels of the organisation, the 'received doctrine' of managerial control can be effective to the degree with which it –

1. Recognises key factors that need control.
2. Establishes standards for measuring achievements.
3. Defines measures of status and performance.
4. Reports and analyses accomplishment by responsibilities.
5. Controls before-the-fact through pre-planning.
6. Highlights important information for managers.
7. Increasingly seeks to observe events that are external to the company, even though in the past they may have been considered as non-quantifiable.

Points to Remember

- **Control** is a comparison and verification process and with the assistance of this process, a balance in the organisation activities that are directed towards the goals that are set can be attained and maintained.

- **Feed forward control** is introducing anticipated problems. As the name proposes, as it occurs before the actual activity, it is future-directed.

- **Concurrent control** or real-time control occurs while altering activities are in progress.

- **Feedback control** takes place, after an activity has taken place.

- **Management control** is the process of ensuring that resources are obtained, used effectively and efficiently in achieving the organisation's objectives.

- **Formal control systems** are written, management-initiated mechanisms that control the behaviour of employees in attaining the organisation's goals.
- **Input controls** are the actions that are taken by the firm before a planned activity is executed.
- **Output control** is used when performance standards are fixed and checked, and the results are assessed.
- A **Management Control System** (MCS) is a set of inter-related communication structures that ease the processing of data to help managers to co-ordinate the parts and achieve the purpose of the organisation on a constant basis.

Questions for Discussion

1. Define the concept of management control. Discuss the nature of control.
2. Why is control a must in business management? What are the requirements of an effective control system?
3. Examine the important features of controlling. What are basic steps in the process of controlling?
4. Define the term 'management control'.
5. What are the distinguishing characteristics of a management control system?
6. Explain the types of management control.
7. What are the elements of management control systems?
8. Discuss the designing of management control systems.
9. Highlight the ten commandments of an effective control system.
10. Explain the factors affecting managerial philosophy.

■■■

Chapter **3**...

Computers Systems

Contents ...

Learning Objectives ...

- To understand the role of computer systems for management control
- To state the need of computers for MIS
- To discuss on computers and information systems
- To explain the types of management support systems
    - (a) Manual Systems
    - (b) Mechanical Systems
    - (c) MIS
    - (d) Decision Support System
    - (e) Expert Systems

3.1 Computers for Management Control Systems

3.1.1 Introduction

With the rising use of computers in business, there is an increasing demand for computer-based management controls which are able to operate in real time. Although there are few examples of real time control systems such as SAGE, SABRE, and PERT, there is by no means wide-scale use of these systems or a basic knowledge of the control process itself. To a certain extent, the majority of computer-based systems can best be explained as "mechanisation" of existing manual systems. To make effective use of computer technology, a body of information is required in management control, feedback theory, information theory, organisation theory and the methods of operations research, management science, computer programming, etc. Therefore, there has been a slow progress in attaining a "designed" computer-based management control systems.

3.1.2 Reasons for Computer-Based Systems for Management Control

One can barely question the difficulty and dynamics of modern organisations. Taking into consideration shorter lead time needs, increased number and complexity of products, wider geographic distribution of customers, and potentially bigger risks in decision-making, management can no longer pay for the luxury of operating on hunch, intuition, or guesswork. To have an effective control, management needs information on time which shows the effect of decisions on the entire business, decision criteria which allow quick response to changing situations, and organisational design based on information needs. When taking the management control problem into consideration, one cannot disregard the question of design of the business itself as an economic system.

Business systems are run by managers who are accountable for organising and utilising the available resources that are dependent on the objectives of owners, and subject to restrictions such as capital structure, physical facilities and market status, so as to guarantee effective operation and existence of the company. Profit maximisation can scarcely be defined as the single business objective; rather, a willingness of the owner to take risks with the inbuilt abilities of the business system which generates a set of reasonable options.

Until of late a methodology has not been available to assess the effect of alternative strategies in a dynamic environment; on the other hand, there are now numerous examples where computer simulation has been used as a research and design tool for this reason.

Computers can be important tool for management control the same way as they are helpful for other applications because of the following reasons.

(i) Speed: In comparison to manual methods, all features of computer operations (except the initial input of manual data via keyboard) occur at very high speeds. Whether the computer is calculating an overhead variance, making an entry in the job cost file, printing an actual budget statement or performing some other job, the computer does it in a very less time.

(ii) Accuracy: All computers include inbuilt checking features which guarantee 100 percent accuracy for all practical purposes in pursuing a programme.

(iii) Filing and retrieval abilities: Computer files always maintain some kind of disk storage; and the connected software file handling systems allow rapid updating, amendment, cross-referencing and recovery of huge amounts of information that would be practically impossible using any manual system.

(iv) Calculations and decision-making ability: Computer calculating speeds are measured in millionths of a second and are the heart of their power.

(v) Input and output facilities: Computers can read and search files, print results or display information on VDU (Visual Display Unit) at very high speeds. With modern software, report layouts can be modified at will, results can be exhibited using various diagrammatic and geographical displays, often in full colour, and displays can be manipulated by the user without leaving his desk.

3.1.3 Importance of Computers for MIS

The study of MIS is not about the use of computers, it is about the provision and use of information that is important to the user. Computers are one important means of generating information and focus on the means of production rather than the requirements of the user that can cause errors. Computers are good at making quick and precise calculations, manipulation, storage and retrieval but are not that good at unforeseen or qualitative work where genuine judgement is needed. It has been recommended that computers can be used to the best advantage for processing data which has the following features.

(a) Number of interacting variables

(b) Speed is an important factor

(c) There are reasonably accurate values

(d) Accuracy of output is important

(e) Operations are repetitive

(f) Large amount of data exist

These features can be related to the requirements of the different management levels as shown below.

Information Characteristics	Presence in Management Information		
	Operational Level	**Tactical Level**	**Strategic Level**
Interacting variables	Frequent ---		Always
Speed important	Usually ---		Rarely
Data accuracy	High ---		Low
Output accuracy	Always --		Rarely
Repetition	Usually ---		Rarely
Data volume	High ---		Low

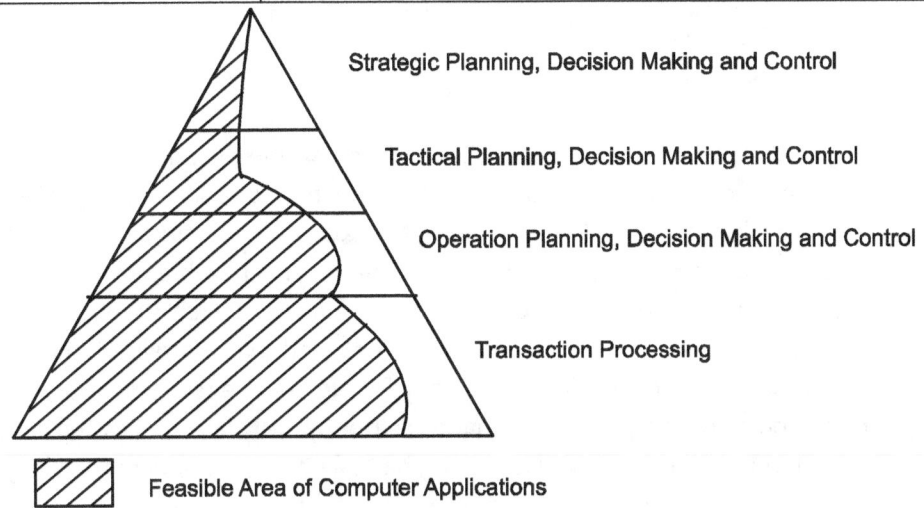

Fig. 3.1: Resulting Applications of Computers

The un-shaded area of Fig. 3.1 shows the unstructured problems and decisions where human participation is important. The separation between computer and human tasks is continuously changing. As software and hardware develop and organisations gain more skill in using computers, the tasks that earlier required managerial expertise and judgement become valuable computer jobs. An example is the extensive use of 'credit scoring' in banks. An applicant for a loan fills a detailed questionnaire and the answers are entered into a computer. The programme performs a series of tests and decides whether or not the loan should be granted. Earlier, all loan applications needed a managerial decision which is now required only for unusual requests, big loans or industrial applications.

3.2 Computers and Information Systems

3.2.1 Introduction

Although the lines between them are blurred and there is a considerable overlap, it is possible to differentiate two major areas of application of computers in information systems.

These are (i) Data Processing (or Transaction Processing) and (ii) Decision Support Systems (or End User Computing). These categories are shown in Fig. 3.2 and developed in the paragraphs below.

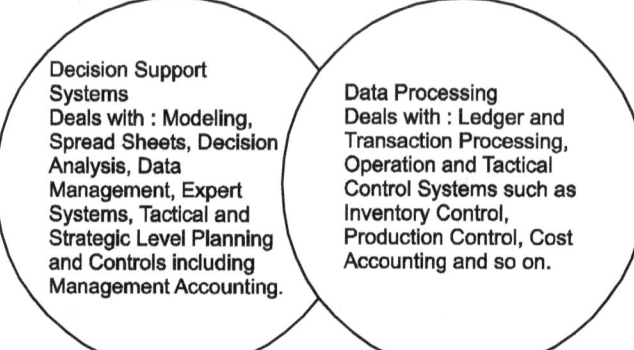

Fig. 3.2: Application of Computers in Information Systems

These systems carry out the important role of collecting and processing everyday transactions of the organisation, thus the other term, transaction processing. Normally these consist of all forms of ledger keeping, accounting receivable and payable, invoicing, credit control, rate demands, stock movements and so on. These kinds of systems were the first to harness the power of the computer and initially were based on centralised mainframe computers. In several cases this still applies, particularly for big volume recurring jobs, but the availability of micro and mini computers has made distribution of data processing feasible and famous. Distributed data has many variations but basically means that data handling and processing are carried out at or near the point of use rather than in one centralised location.

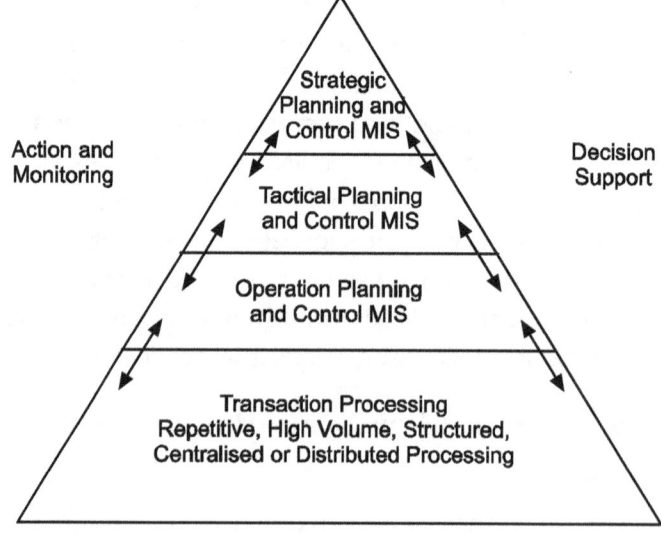

Fig. 3.3: Transaction Processing as a Base for MIS

Transaction processing is considerably more important in terms of processing time, volume of input and output than say, information production for tactical and strategic planning. Transaction processing is important to keep the operations of the organisation running efficiently and provides the base for all other internal information's support. This is shown in Fig. 3.3.

3.2.2 Types of Management Support Systems: Generation of Information Systems

There are six separate types or generations of information systems – (1) Manual Systems (2) Mechanical Systems, (3) Electronic Data Processing (EDP) Systems, (4) Management Information Systems, (5) Decision Support Systems, (6) Expert Systems. The term generation is used because these information systems are developed in a natural order, and each can be said to characterise a data processing period. On the other hand, these generations of information systems do not match with the generations of computer hardware, and, more significantly, each type of information system is still lucrative today in the 'right' application. Table 3.1 summarises the features of each type of information system.

3.2.3 Manual Systems

The business information systems that were used before were manual information systems, whose basic tools were pens, pencils, index cards, columnar tablets, accounting ledgers and filing cabinets. A recent example would be a manual grade book of students' examination records maintained by a trainer.

In the past, manual systems in business settings also had a high potential for clerical and technical mistakes. This created major barriers for preparing reports of financial statements and caused companies to avoid preparing less-demand reports altogether. Thus in manual systems, the data that is required for decision-making was in the system, but there were no lucrative processes available to prepare it for managerial uses.

3.2.4 Mechanical Systems

In the beginning, in 1890 with the addition of machines, sorting trays, and unit record equipment (that is, card-processing equipment), companies were capable of substituting mechanical process for manual procedures. These devices facilitated data processing, improved computational accurateness, and reduced the time needed to prepare reports. Like manual systems, mechanical systems focussed on the processing of information rather than the informational requirements of managers, that is, they focus on the efficiency of data processing rather than data processing effectiveness.

3.2.5 Electronic Data Processing (EDP) Systems

The first computerised applications (1953-1965) were essentially automated manuals or mechanical systems that merely computerised earlier processing techniques. This approach was reasonable since these systems were what a company best understood and what employees best knew how to function. These systems are known as Electronic Data Processing (EDP) systems or transaction processing systems. The first EDP systems were entirely batch-oriented. Early EDP systems concentrated on volume-oriented applications and were first implemented in those applications that followed well-defined processing rules. These twin contemplations of high transaction volumes and well-defined rules made accounting applications among the most 'natural' ones to computerise and assist in describing why many of the first computer employees started their careers in accounting departments.

3.2.6 Management Information Systems (MISs)

As noted earlier, one of the key deficiencies of early information system was their incapability to give useful managerial reports EDP systems, but the fact that EDP systems were essentially automated manual systems and they concentrated on operational detail, not managerially-oriented overviews. Also as most of the early EDP systems used batch processing, managers had to wait until the required reports were produced during their regular cycles. The development of management information systems or MISs in the late 1960s and early 1970s was in reply to the need for managerial information rather than a detailed, transactions information. To design a useful MIS, thus, was significant to know the four information requirements of managers, mainly information that is – (i) timely, (ii) accurate, (iii) complete, and (iv) concise.

A business information system achieves the first three of these by using computer hardware, software, and procedure for computational precision, and by installing controls that guarantee the complete collection, reading, and processing of data. MIS excels over EDP systems is in its ability to produce management information in brief, useful formats. Examples of managerial reports that meet this goal consist of:

1. Summary reports that deliberately leave out details in favour of activity summaries.
2. Demand reports that are made only when a manager needs them.
3. Exception reports include the output that satisfies fixed 'exception' conditions, for example, report showing only those accounts receivable more than 90 days past due.
4. Custom reports that are customised to managerial specifications.

MISs also support online files that allow managers to access information that is of immediate interest and report generators that allow managers to design their own reports, for instance, electronic spreadsheets or data base management systems.

Another issue with EDP systems was that managers often required comparative information that EDP systems were not capable of storing easily in a single file. For instance, an EDP system might store the information of employee health coverage in one file and the information of employee absenteeism in another file. The independence of these two files made it difficult to make a single report that included information from both. MISs improved this circumstance by incorporating file information in the online data bases that was made possible by the development of hard disks and data base management system. With these instruments, MISs were capable of meeting informational requirements with more desirable printed reports and online access and retrieval.

Table 3.1: Six Generations of Information Systems

	Manual Systems	Mechanical Systems	EDP Systems	Manage-ment Infor-mation Systems (MIS)	Decision Support	Expert Systems
1. Time span	Before 1900	1900-1953	1953-1965	1965-1975	1975 to present	1975 to present
2. Primary functions	All users before mechanic-cal systems	All users before computers	1. Automatic record keeping 2. Volume data processing	Provide relevant information to manage-ment	Assist decision makers with unstructured problems	Assist users requiring expert opinions on complex matters
3. File orient-tation	Manual files	Mechanical sequential files (for example, card files)	Sequential files updated in batch	Online, direct access files, often in data bases	User-created files often on micro computers	Knowledge data bases and large programs containing detailed processing logic
4. Type of data processing	Manual	Mechanical (for example, with unit record equipment)	Batch	Mixture of batch and real time	Almost exclusively interactive real time	Interactive using programs, employing artificial intelligence
5. Primary users	All users before mecha-nical systems	All users before computers	Operational level employees	Middle managers	Top management	Specialist requiring expert opinions
6. Types of decision-making	All decisions	All decisions	Operational decisions	Tactical decisions	Strategic (policy) decisions	Expert decisions
7. Types of reports	Minimal	Transaction detailed listings	Transaction detailed listings	Summary reports, exception reports	Customs-designed reports	Specific to the type of expert system

3.2.7 Decision Support Systems (DSSs)

Decision support systems are information processing systems that are often used by accountants, executives and managers for support in decision-making. It needs a combination of advanced hardware technology, reciprocal computing design, graphic capabilities and user-friendly software.

Abbreviated, the term refers to an interactive computerised system that collects and presents information from an extensive range of sources, normally for business reasons. DSS applications are systems and subsystems that assist individuals in making decisions based on data that is gathered from various sources.

For instance, a national on-line bookseller desires to start selling its products in the global market but first needs to decide if that will be a sensible business decision. The vendor can use a DSS to collect information from its own resources to decide if the firm has the capability to increase its business and also from external resources, such as industry information, to decide if there is indeed a demand to meet. The DSS will gather and analyse the information and then present it in a way that can be translated by the people. Some decision support systems come very close to acting as artificial intelligence agents.

DSS applications are not single information resources, such as a database or a program that graphically represents sales figures, but the combination of integrated resources functioning together.

3.2.7.1 Characteristics of Decision Support Systems

1. **Supports Management Decision-making**
   - It supports decision-making at different levels of management.
   - Operational managers can use DSS for decisions of scheduling jobs.
   - Top-level managers can use DSS for taking policy decisions like continuing or discontinuing a product.
   - While the system may point to a specific decision, it is the user who finally makes the final choice.

2. **Solves Unstructured Problems**
   - It is used to analyse those problems that do not have simple solution procedures but those problems for which managerial judgement is required as well as structured analysis.
   - The user will have to use query DSS, use his judgement, imagination and discretion to get the best out of a DSS. For instance, future interest rates, market demand, competitor's decision and action etc.
   - "What if" query modules assist in using permutation and combinations of input data to get all possible predictions, which might happen in the future for which decisions are made now.
   - Although system designers may develop DSS for one time use, managers use the DSS to solve specific type of problem on a regular basis.

3. **Friendly Computer Interface**

- Since the users are non-programmers, the system has to be user-friendly that contains interactive software.
- The availability of non-procedural languages facilitates the communication between the user and the DSS.

3.2.7.2 Components of Decision Support Systems

1. **The User**
   (a) The user of a DSS is generally a manager with a problem looking for a best solution.
   (b) The managers may be at different levels in the organisation, namely, operational, top management or financial etc.
   (c) The user does not need to have extensive education in computer programming, but they should have detailed understanding of the problem and the factors to be taken into consideration in finding a solution.
   (d) A planning language is a non-procedural, simple to use and takes care of the step-by-step solution to a problem. Thus the users can focus on what should be achieved rather than how the computer carries out each step.

2. **Databases**
   (a) DSS consists of one or more databases, both routine and on-routine and from both internal and external sources.
   (b) External database includes data about economic conditions, market demands, levels of competition etc.
   (c) The DSS users may make their own databases by integrating different other databases from other areas such as marketing, production and personnel etc.

3. **Planning Language**
   The two types of planning language are as follows.
   (a) **General purpose:** These planning languages enable the user to carry out routine tasks like retrieving information from all existing database for statistical analysis.
   (b) **Special purpose:** These planning languages enable the user to deal with a broad range of budgeting, forecasting functions and they are limited in what they do. They can do particular jobs better than the general purpose planning language.

4. **Model Base**
   (a) The model base is the "brain" of the DSS since it performs data manipulations and computations with the information given to it by the user and the database.
   (b) There are different model bases, which are application based or tailored for giving the best decision-making models.
   (c) They could be based on mathematical, statistical or financial based functions and formulations or a combination of all of them to give results with the input of the user.

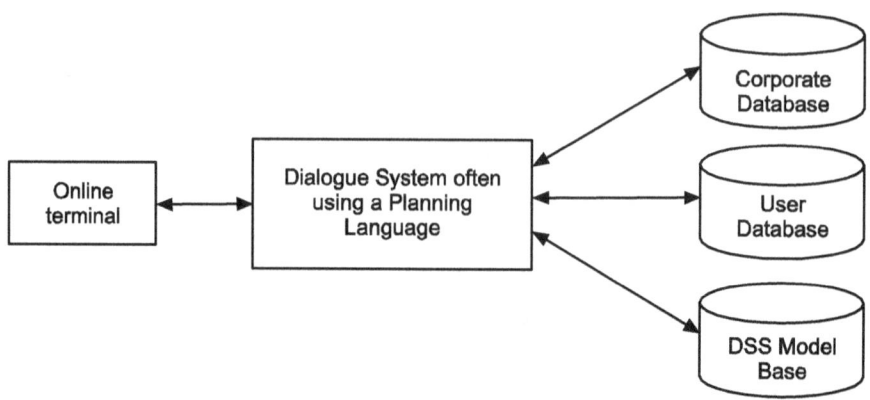

Fig. 3.4: Decision Support System

3.2.7.3 Criteria for Use of DSS

DSSs are man/machine systems and are appropriate for semi-structured problems. The problem should be significant to the manager and the decision needed must be an important one. Besides, if an interactive computer-based system is to be used then some of the following criteria should be met.

1. **There should be a large database:** A database is a collection of structured data with a minimum replication of information. The database is common to all users of the system but is independent of the programmes which use the data. If the database is too big for searching manually then a computer-supported approach might be valuable.

2. **Larger amount of computation or data manipulation:** Where the analysis of the problem needs substantial computation or data manipulation, computing power will probably be advantageous.

3. **Complex inter-relationships:** Where there is a big database or where there are a number of factors involved it is often hard to evaluate all the possible inter-relationships without the help of a computer.

4. **Analysis by stages:** Where the problem is interactive with stages for review and re-evaluation, it becomes harder to deal with it manually. The computer-based model can answer the question 'what if?'

5. **Judgement required:** In difficult circumstances judgement is required both to decide the problem and the solution; without help, no computer system can provide this.

6. **Communication:** Where many individuals are involved in the problem-solving process, each contributing some special skill, then the synchronising power of the computer can be of help.

It follows from the above criteria that DSS are unsuitable for unstructured problems and unnecessary for complete structured problems because these can be dealt with completely by the computer and man/machine communication is pointless. In outline, DSS needs a database, the software to handle database and decision support programmes including modeling, spread sheet and analysis packages, expert systems and so on.

3.2.7.4 Where to Apply DSS

DSSs are successful in companies of medium to big size and in decision scenarios needing in-depth analysis of internal and external data. The success of DSS significantly, depends on top management support, regularity and length of use, training of managers and variety of decision-making situations.

If the business process is easy and repetitive in nature, DSS may not be capable of justifying its costs. DSS applied to structured decisions only increase costs and confusion. DSSs have been found to be helpful in decision areas where flexibility in data and modelling is needed for better decision-making. The usual areas of application of DSS in production and finance functions of business are.

1. **Production:** Procurement analysis, cost estimation and analysis, production planning and scheduling, make or buy decisions, inventory planning and control, manpower loading, etc.

2. **Accounting Information Systems (AISs):** Decision support systems are extensively used as part of an organisation's Accounting Information Systems (AISs); the difficulty and the nature may differ. Many DSSs are developed in-house using either a generalised type of DSS or a spreadsheet programme to solve particular issues. The different DSS applications in AIS are as under:

    (a) Capital Budgeting System
    *   Firms need new tools to assess high technology investment decisions.
    *   Net Present Value (NPV), Internal Rate of Return (IRR) etc. are a number of tools that are available for taking decisions on investment. For example, the Automan model enables the users to take into consideration the financial, non-financial qualifications and quantitative factors that are to be included in their decision-making process. Many options are offered by the DSS.
    *   Many investment options can be assessed at once.

    (b) Cost Accounting System
    *   Managing the costs in every industry needs controlling of costs of raw materials, expensive machinery, technology and staff etc.
    *   This system provides calculation of the cost of production of different products and services.
    *   Cost accounting Decision Support Systems can be mixed with other segments of accounting for fixing the selling prices, budgeting for the next year, etc.
    *   They can be used for making or buying decision, optimal product mix etc. which are based upon the cost of production, demand of the products in the market etc.

    (c) Budget Variance Analysis System
    *   Establishments use computerised DSSs to produce periodic variance reports, create budget forecasts etc.
    *   The DSS thus assists the controllers in creating and controlling budgets for the cost centre managers reporting to them.

Table 3.2: Difference between DSS and MIS

Dimensions	DSS	MIS
Focus	Analysis, decision support	Information processing
Typical Users Served	Analysts, professions, managers (via intermediaries)	Middle, lower levels, sometime senior executives
Impetus	Effectiveness	Efficiency
Application	Diversified areas where managerial decisions are made	Production control, sales forecasts, financial analysis, human resource management
Database(s)	Special	Corporate
Decision Support Capabilities	Supports semi-structured and unstructured decision-making; mainly ad hoc, but sometimes repetitive decisions	Direct or indirect support, mainly structured routine problems, using standard operations, research and other models
Type of Information	Information to support specific situations	Scheduled and demand reports; structured flow, exception reporting mainly internal operations
Principal Use	Planning, organising, staffing and control	Control
Adaptability to Individual User	Permits individual judgement, what-if capabilities, some choice of dialogue style	Usually none, standardised
Graphics	Integrated part of many DSSs	Desirable
User Friendliness	A must where no intermediaries are used	Desirable
Treatment of Information	Information provided by the EIS/or MIS is used as an input to the DSS	Information is provided to a diversified group of users who then manipulate it or summarise it as needed
Supporting Detailed Information	Can be programmed into DSS	Inflexibility of reports, cannot get the supporting details quickly
Model Base	The core of the DSS	Standard models are available but are not managed
Construction	By users, either alone or with specialists from IS or IC departments.	By vendors or IS specialists
Hardware	Mainframes, micros or distributed	Mainframes, micros or distributed
Nature of Computing Packages	Large computational capabilities, modeling languages and simulation, applications and DSS generators	Application oriented, performance reports, strong reporting capabilities, standard statistical, financial, accounting and management science models

3.2.8 Expert Systems

The increasing difficulties and dynamism in the upcoming business environment needs greater communication of functional managers with the specialists in order to get timely advice. These experts would not only shift information from huge pools of different data, but also use their skills to offer advice.

Conventionally, the expertise available in an organisation has given a significant basis for attaining, improving and maintaining its competitive position. All other things being equal, companies without comparable knowledge are at a disadvantage.

Human experts may not be capable of coping with the new challenges, given the restrictions of time and difficulties of the new environment. In addition, there may not be consistency of advice for a given decision situation over a period.

This is due to the obvious incapability of individuals to capture the effect of different decision variables all the time. The Information Fatigue Syndrome and the limitations of human experts in the altering business environment have resulted in increasing popularity of expert systems.

These systems simulate human activity and keep capturing and systematising business knowledge, expanding the decision-making capabilities of costly and limited human experts, so that others can use their decision experiences. They offer the advantage of flexibility in capturing and representing information of different types in different forms.

An expert system receives a problem from the user, recognises its data needs, analyses the relevant data against the decision rules that are included in a knowledge system. Once the problem is resolved, the system through its inference engine reports the solution to the user and is also capable of explaining its line of logic in reaching that solution.

An expert system can act as an aid to managerial effectiveness by giving advice. Its solutions/advices are always reliable, uniform, detailed and systematic. It works as a standardised problem-solver.

A user can study the underlying principle and is free to accept, alter or refuse the solution. Unlike other expert systems in the field of medicine, engineering, etc. the purpose of the business expert system is not to substitute assessment by human expert(s) by the computer program.

Rather, the goal is to obtain the skills of the human expert and make it available in a standardised form to human expert(s) and others in the organisation. They work out strategies to use information in the application areas so as to develop reasonable solutions to the problems.

Expert systems are computer programmes that try to capture the experience, decision rules, and thought processes of experts in a particular area. Such systems are frequently helpful to managers in remote locations who do not have access to external experts, to companies that cannot pay for full-time consultants, to organisations that need the same experts at many places simultaneously, to companies whose experts leave or retire, or to experts themselves who want second opinions.

- Expert systems are formed by interviewing professionals and on serving how they work, to know how they reason and answer. Consequently, expert systems frequently use artificial intelligence, that is, computer programmes that rouse the thought processes of humans.

- When modelling these processes, some expert systems use 'decision tree structures', that is, networks of it that allows a system to arrive at conclusions through the process of removal. This is known as forward reasoning, or forward chaining, and contracts with those expert systems that begin with evidence and work backward to decide causes, that is, backward chaining.

- Expert systems are like decision support systems in that both attempt to give meaningful data for decision-making proposals and both generally use interactive computer systems to facilitate user dialogues.

- Expert systems are not like decision support systems in that expert systems highlight structured problems, generally need specific information for input and are often not capable of exploring 'what-if' scenarios. However, expert systems hold great promise for technical and managerial decision-making because of their abilities to capture years of expert experience and to discover millions of unrelated possibilities.

The application areas of expert systems differ extensively. Medical diagnosis, geological exploration, and process control applications are predominantly common. Several expert systems are also expensive to maintain because they run on special computers, because new data must be entered to keep existing databases, and because they must be monitored regularly to ensure they are solving problems properly. These high maintenance costs cause firms to discard projects even after sinking thousands of rupees into them. In recent times, new software tools have been declared that would decrease development time and costs significantly. Examples of such tools are Expert systems Environment/VM (IBM), VM programming in logic (IBM), AI Vacstation (DEC), OPSS Expert System Development Language (DEC), Quintus Prolog (DEC), LISP/VE (CDC) and Knowledge Engineering System/VE (DEC), Expert System "shells" or software packages have also been developed for micro computers, although there is some dispute whether such packages are able to develop 'true' expert systems.

Table 3.3: Examples of Expert Systems

Name	Application area	Uses
CADUCEUS	Medicine	Diagnosing medical problems from symptoms
Capital Investments	Investment	Making capital investment decisions
DELTA	Machine maintenance	Maintaining locomotives
DENDRAL	Chemistry	Outlining the molecular structures of organic compounds
Dip Meter Advisor	Geological exploration	Analysing geological data from oil dipmetres
MUDMAN	Geological exploration	Analysing 'mud' extract from an oil shaft for content
MYCIN	Medicine	Diagnosing and treating bacterial infections
ONCOCIN	Medicine	Analysing medical symptoms for cancer
Prospector R-1	Geological exploration computers	Locating mineral deposits; designing computer systems for customers
STEAMER	Training in the navy	Training boiler room technicians
XCON	Computers	Evaluating a computer to make sure that it has correct parts.
XSELL	Computers	Fitting computer hardware and soft ware to customer requirements

Benefits of Expert Systems

1. **Coding of expertise:** The important advantage of business expert system is that it assists in formalising/codifying the reasoning ability of an organisation. While developing BES, lot of attempts were made to represent expertise in the form of rules, frames, cases, text and graphs.

   This leads to compilation of information concerning the expertise until now held confidently by the experts. Such a store of skill can give a basis for better training of human experts in the organisation in addition to leading to better decision-making.

2. **Enhanced understanding of business process:** It improves the understanding of the decision-making process that may consecutively bring about improvement in the

process. During the development process, the existing ways of decision-making are recognised and reviewed. This helps in improving the decision-making process. Frequent communication of experts with BES is a great learning process and results in joint improvement of each other's problem-solving capabilities.

3. **Timely availability of expertise:** BES is capable of providing expertise when a human expert is not available. These systems do not have problems of availability that is quite common among human experts. BESs are available to users for consultations at unusual hours, have no previous engagements, do not go on leave for one reason or the other and do not resign from the company to join a competitor.

4. **Easy replication:** The marginal cost of replicating a BES is unimportant. Once a BES is doing well at one place, it can be replicated at other places having similar decision-making environments, without loss of time or opportunity.

5. **Eliminates routine consultation requests:** BES can assist a human expert in decreasing his work load by directing the routine type of consultation requests to BES. This allows the human expert to focus on more challenging problems that are not solved by BES.

6. **Consistency:** BES offers consistent advice on problems. Their advice does not suffer from ignoring some factors, not remembering some of the steps, personal bias or temperamental problems.

7. **Line of logic:** BES offers a line of logic used along with the solution. This allows the manager to importantly look at the solutions and find out whether the line of logic used is suitable or not. This helps the manager in knowing the strength and weaknesses of the solution and implement his business judgement to reach decisions.

8. **Strategic applications:** The advantages of BES help in product and service differentiation and decreased costs. They also help to develop niche markets where competitors without such systems may not be efficient. Thus, BESs can provide the strategic edge to a company.

Points to Remember

- In **manual systems**, the data that is required for decision-making was in the system, but there were no lucrative processes available to prepare it for managerial uses

- **Mechanical systems** focussed on the processing of information rather than the informational requirements of managers, that is, they focus on the efficiency of data processing rather than data processing effectiveness.

- The first computerised applications (1953-1965) were essentially automated manuals or mechanical systems that merely computerised earlier processing techniques. This approach was reasonable since these systems were what a company best understood and what employees best knew how to function. These systems are known as **Electronic Data Processing (EDP)** systems or transaction processing systems.

- The development of **management information systems** or MISs was in reply to the need for managerial information rather than a detailed, transactions information. MIS is significant to know the four information requirements of managers, mainly information that is – (i) timely, (ii) accurate, (iii) complete, and (iv) concise.

- **Decision support systems** refers to an interactive computerised system that collects and presents information from an extensive range of sources, normally for business reasons

- An **expert system** receives a problem from the user, recognises its data needs, analyses the relevant data against the decision rules that are included in a knowledge system. Once the problem is resolved, the system through its inference engine reports the solution to the user and is also capable of explaining its line of logic in reaching that solution.

Questions for Discussion

1. What are the role computer systems for management control?
2. State the need of computers for MIS.
3. Discuss on computers and information systems.
4. Explain the types of management support systems:
   (a) Manual systems
   (b) Mechanical systems
   (c) MIS
   (d) Decision support system
   (e) Expert systems
5. In what ways are manual information systems and mechanical information systems similar? In what ways are they different?
6. What are management information systems (MISs)? How are they better than EDP systems? In what ways are they same as EDP systems?
7. Describe decision support systems (DSSs). What are the major components? How are they used? How are they similar to management information systems? How are they different?
8. What is an expert system? Why are there so few of them today? Why are more expected?

■■■

Chapter 4...

Management Control of Projects

Contents ...

Learning Objectives ...

- To explain the aspects of project and factors affecting project
- To discuss the three dimensions in project planning- time, cost, and quality dimension
- To understand the concept of project control
- To discuss reports on cost and time, revisions and project evaluation

4.1 Project

4.1.1 Meaning of Project

A project is a set of activities meant to achieve a specified end result of sufficient significance to be of interest to the management of an organisation. Projects consist of construction projects, the production of a sizable unique product (such as turbine), rearranging a plant, developing and marketing a new product, consulting engagement, audits, acquisitions and divestitures, litigation, financial restructuring, research and development work, development and installation of information systems and many others.

An assignment starts when management has accepted the general nature of what has to be finished and has authorised the estimated quantity of resources that are to be spent in undertaking this work. The assignment ends when its objective has been achieved, for example, completion of the construction of a building, completion of a development project may lead to an operation that is in progress.

4.1.2 Overall Nature of the Problem

Project management concentrates on achieving a specific end result, that is, the successful completion of the project. Management control of projects thus varies from that of responsibility centres in two aspects.

1. In a project, the concentration is on the work involved in producing the end item irrespective of which responsibility centres take part in this work, whereas in a responsibility centre the concentration is on all the work completed by that responsibility centre.

2. In a project, the time period of interest is the time used in the whole project, whereas in a responsibility centre the time period of interest is a calendar period, such as a month.

The above two differences lead to a very different control procedure for projects than that of incomplete operations/responsibility centres.

4.1.3 Aspects of Project

1. **Objectives:** A project has a set of objectives or a mission. Once the objectives are attained the project is completed.

2. **Life cycle:** A project has a lifecycle. The lifecycle includes five stages, that is, conception stage, definition stage, planning and organising stage, implementation stage and commissioning stage.

3. **Uniqueness:** Every project is unique and no two projects are the same. Setting up a cement factory and construction of a highway are two different projects having unique characteristics.

4. **Teamwork:** Project is a teamwork and it typically includes different areas. There will be employees' specialised in their individual areas and co-ordination among the different areas calls for teamwork.

5. **Complexity:** A project is a difficult set of activities relating to different areas.

6. **Risk and uncertainty:** Risk and uncertainty go together with the project. Risk-free only means that the element is not actually noticeable on the surface and it will be hidden underneath.

7. **Customer specific nature:** A project is always customer specific. It is the customer who determines upon the product to be produced or services to be offered and thus it is the responsibility of any organisation to go for projects/services that will match the customer requirements.

8. **Change:** Changes happen all through the lifespan of a project as a natural result of many environmental factors. The changes may differ from minor changes, which may have very little effect on the project, to major changes which may have a big effect or even may alter the nature of the project.

9. **Optimality:** A project always aims to optimally use resources for the overall development of the economy.

10. **Sub-contracting:** A high level of work in a project is completed through contractors. The more the difficulty of the project, the more will be the extent of contracting.

11. **Unity in diversity:** A project is a complex set of thousands of varieties. The varieties are in terms of technology, tools and materials, machinery and people, work, culture and others.

4.1.4 Factors Affecting Project

Identifying a new valuable project is a difficult problem. It involves careful study from many different angles. Following are the factors that have an effect on project.

1. **Performance of existing industries:** Performance of existing industries provides a good indication about the health of a particular industry. An analysis of the profitability and break-even point of different industries will provide sufficient information about the financial health of different industrial sectors. Though these provide an overall picture of industrial health, one should not be simply carried away by the present performance alone. One should be clever enough to read the phase of business cycle in which the different industries stand at a specific time. For instance, a specific industrial sector might be performing well, but it might have already crossed its saturation phase and might have already fallen into the decline stage of its business cycle. Entering into such an industry will prove to be disastrous. In the same way, the financial performance of another industrial sector that is not so motivating might have the potential to grow quickly, as the industry is only in the initial stage of its business cycle. Before making a final choice, such factors should be carefully analysed.

2. **Availability of raw materials:** Easy availability of good quality raw materials at lesser prices is a definite sign that some projects that can make use of those raw materials may be through of. For example, in an area where agriculture is the main activity and where agricultural products are available in plenty, the potential can be made use of by establishing food processing industries. Availability of minerals may cause a rise in chemical industries.

3. **Availability of skilled labour:** Based on the locally available skilled labour force, suitable industries that can make better use of the skilled manpower can be recognised.

4. **Import/export statistics:** Import/export statistics may disclose the potential that remain untapped. Higher proportion of import of a specific product and increasing trend in its import shows that a product, which can serve as an import substitute can be produced locally. In the same way, higher proportion of export of a specific product and increasing trend in its export shows high export potential for the product.

5. **Price trend:** The trend in the price of different products/services may give an indication about the demand-supply relationship. If the general price level is increasing during the past few years and if the increase in price level of a specific product is steeper than the rise in price level, it may show a demand-supply gap. Additionally, a detailed study may be undertaken to determine the extent of demand-supply gap.

6. **Data from various sources:** Various publications of government, banks and financial institutions, consultancy organisations, manufacturer's associations, export promotion councils, research institutions and international agencies have information and statistics which may indicate potential ventures. A study of the working results and balance sheets of existing firms is helpful in understanding the sectors of industry that are doing well. Study of profitability, break-even level, earnings per share (EPS) of different industries may indicate those industries where opportunities exist for new investments.

7. **Research laboratories:** Research laboratories that are involved in recognising new products/processes frequently provide new avenues or commercial exploitation. On the other hand, proper care should be taken before trying to go for large scale production of products that have been proved in the laboratory to guarantee that conditions under which the products are developed in the laboratory can be simulated in the actual production line also. Failure to accurately simulate laboratory conditions may cause failure when the product is produced in a big scale.

8. **Consumption abroad:** Those businessmen who are ready to take higher risks can recognise projects for the manufacture of goods or supply of services which are new to the country, but widely used abroad. Thus, observing the consumption pattern abroad will help in recognising projects with export potential.

9. **Identifying unfulfilled psychological needs:** For groups that are well established, there may be unsatisfied psychological needs, though the physical needs of the consumers might have been fulfilled. Consumer goods like cosmetics, bathing soaps, toothpastes etc., come under this group. New products of this group being introduced and accepted by the consumers show the unfulfilled psychological needs of the consumers.

10. **Plan outlays and government guidelines:** The government plays a significant role in the economy of a country. The government's plan of outlays in different sectors gives useful indicators towards possible investment opportunities. They show the potential demand for goods and services by the different sectors of the economy. The department of industrial development, government of India, publishes guidelines to industries annually which is an important source of information to recognise the scope for new investments. This publication gives information about production performance of different sectors of industries, the licensed and installed capacity, scope for future exports, location and structure of industries etc.

11. **Analysis of economic and social trends:** An analysis of the economic and social trends of the society will be very useful in recognising and projecting the demands for different goods and services. For example, the growing desire for leisure points to investment opportunity in recreational activities, rest-houses, resorts etc. The growing awareness of the value of time points to growing demands for fast-foods, high-speed vehicles, better mode of transport, ready-made garments etc.

12. **Possibility of reviving sick units:** In any economy there are several industrial units that might have become sick, that are becoming sick, that are on the verge of death and that are weak. An industry that has become weak/sick might still have the capacity to become economically feasible provided the reason for the weakness/sickness are simply because of factors that are internal to the organisation. A promising entrepreneur who has the required entrepreneurial skills can take over a weak/sick unit and restore it. The infusion of extra capital, provision of complementary inputs, revamping the organisational structure etc. are some of the corrective measures that are required to be completed to nurse an ailing industrial unit and to bring it back to life.

4.2 Project Planning

4.2.1 Introduction

In the planning phase, the project planning team considers the estimates as a starting point to be used as a basis for the decision to carry out the project. It refines these estimates into detailed specifications and schedules for the product and a cost budget. It also develops a management control system and underlying task control systems and an organisation chart. The boxes on this organisation chart are slowly filled with the names of employees who are to supervise the work.

Project planning defines the project activities and end products that will be carried out and describe how the activities can be completed. The reason for project planning is to define each task, estimate the time and resources needed, and provide a framework for management review and control. The project planning activities and goals include defining:

- The particular work to be performed and goals that define and bind the project.
- Estimates to be documented for planning, tracking, and controlling the project.
- Commitments that are planned, documented, and agreed to by affected groups.
- Project alternatives, assumptions, and constraints.

The planning process comprises of steps to estimate the size of the project, the technical scope of the effort, the resources needed to finish the project, produce a schedule, recognise and evaluate risks, and negotiate commitments.

Repetition of these steps is required to establish the project plan. Normally, many iterations of the planning process are carried out before a plan is actually finished.

4.2.2 Product Planning: The Three Constraints

The three constraints in a project management triangle are time, cost and scope.

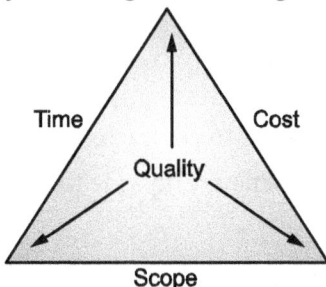

Fig. 4.1

1. **Time:** A project's activities can either take a short or a long time to complete. Completion of tasks depends on numerous factors such as the number of people working on the project, experience, skills, etc.

Time is an important factor which is uncontrollable. However, failure to meet the deadlines in a project can create bad effects. Most frequently, the main reason for organisations to fail in terms of time is because of lack of resources.

2. **Cost:** When undertaking a project, it's very important for both the project manager and the organisation to have an estimated cost. Budgets will guarantee that the project is developed or implemented below a certain cost.

   At times, project managers have to give out additional resources in order to meet the deadlines with a penalty of additional project costs.

3. **Scope:** Scope looks at the result of the project undertaken. This includes a list of deliverables, which is required to be addressed by the project team.

   A successful project manager will know to manage both the scope of the project and any change in scope which has an effect on time and cost.

Quality

Quality is not a part of the project management triangle, but it is the final objective of every delivery. Thus, the project management triangle represents implied quality.

Several project managers are under the view that 'high quality comes with high cost', which to some degree is true. By using substandard resources to achieve project deadlines does not guarantee success of the overall project.

Like with the scope, quality will also be a significant deliverable for the project.

4.2.3 Time Dimensions in Project Planning: Scheduling

Scheduling is nothing but the arrangement of activities of the project in the order of time in which they are to be performed.

Logical sequence of events would be as under:

- Land acquisition.
- Site development.
- Preparing building plans, estimates, designs, getting necessary approvals and entrusting the construction work to contractors.
- Construction of building, machinery foundation and other related civil works and completion of the same.
- Placing order for the machinery.
- Receipt of machinery at site.
- Erection of machinery.
- Commissioning of plant and taking trial runs.
- Commencement of regular commercial production.

Each of the above mentioned activities use resources, namely, time, money and effort. The sequence of activities should be so planned as to reduce the amount of resource that is being consumed. As a part of technical appraisal, the financial establishments call for a detailed project implementation schedule showing the different steps to be taken up in the project implementation in chorological order and the time needed for completing each phase.

Network Analysis Techniques

I.   Scheduling Techniques

All activities use resources of three types namely, time, men and materials. The project scheduling methods are concerned with the resource 'time'. One of the goals of project management is to optimise the use of resources. Scheduling techniques provide different solutions to optimise the project time.

1.   Bar Charts

A bar chart is a pictorial representation indicating the different activities that are involved in a project. The chart has two co-ordinate axes, one axis represents the activities and the other axis represents the time needed for completing the individual activities. The bar chart was first developed by Henry L. Gantt and hence referred as the Gantt Chart.

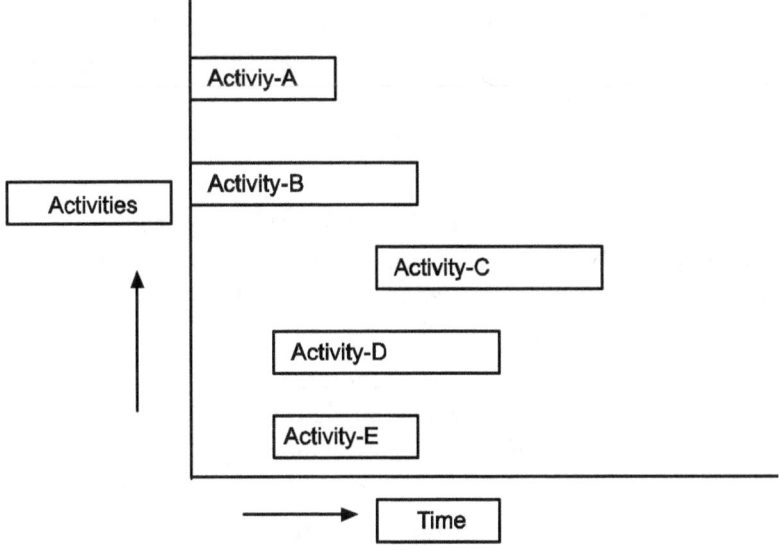

Fig. 4.2: Bar Chart

In the axis that represents activities that can be taken at the same time, while some activities can be considered only after completing some activities. There may be also some activities which are independent of other activities.

Consider the example of construction of a residential house. The following are some of the activities involved in the construction of a residential building.

Activities	Time required
Digging of foundation	3 weeks
Pouring foundation concrete	1 week
Construction of walls	10 weeks
Construction of roof slab	3 weeks
Fixing of doors and windows	1 week
Digging of well	1 week
Plastering and finishing of walls	2 weeks

The above chart can be shown in a bar chart after identifying their logical sequence. If water needed for the construction work is not available at the project site, the activity "digging of well" takes priority. If however, the water needed for the construction work can be acquired without much difficulty, digging of well can be postponed to a later date and it need not be the starting activity.

Limitations of Bar Chart

Limitations of bar chart are as follows –

(a) Bar charts are difficult to update when there are many changes.

(b) When there are changes between the plan and the actual achievement, bar charts rapidly become outdated.

(c) Bar charts do not equate time with cost hence time-cost relationship cannot be derived from them.

(d) Bar charts do not provide methods for optimising allocation.

(e) Considering the above limitation, bar charts are useful only for smaller projects and cannot be effectively used for medium sized and large projects.

2. Programme-Progress Charts

The bar chart discussed in the previous paragraph depicts the proposed activities of a project with their estimated time duration. A bar chart is drawn to have a pictorial view of the logical sequence of operations and their inter-relationships and to have an estimate as to when the project will be completed. It is only a projection in the future.

A programme-progress chart is also a bar-chart; but apart from showing the activities with their proposed time, this chart also integrates the actual progress of the different activities. Both the estimated time and the actual time taken for completing different activities are included in the programme-progress chart. This chart helps in understanding the time lag between the estimated and actual progress of work during implementing the project.

II. Network Based Scheduling

For bigger projects involving numerous activities, project scheduling becomes very difficult and the use of traditional techniques of scheduling will likely result in either under-estimation or over-estimation of project implementation period, both of which will have serious results. If the time of completing the project is under-estimated, the actual implementation period will be more than the estimated period of time resulting in 'time over-run'. Invariably time over-run leads to cost over-run of projects. If the additional costs are not made available in time, there will be a delay in completing the project.

Network-based scheduling of projects helps in solving difficult project scheduling problems.

There are network scheduling techniques. They are –

(a) Critical Path Method (CPM) and

(b) Programme Evaluation Review Technique (PERT)

(a) Critical Path Method (CPM): A network represents the logical sequence of activities included in a project. The activities are represented by arrows and arrows flow from the left to right. In a network, there are several paths starting from the initial event and leading to the last event. If the duration of all activities that lie on a specific path is added, it gives the duration of that path. Each path in a network will have a different time. The path that has the longest duration is called the critical path and the activities that lie on the critical path are called critical activities. It is the critical path that fixes the overall duration of the project. For instance, if there are five paths in a network and if the duration of these paths are 15 weeks, 13 weeks, 14 weeks, 25 weeks and 26 weeks respectively, the path having 26 weeks duration is the critical path. This represents that the project duration is 26 weeks. Though other paths in the network have duration less than 26 weeks, the project will be finished in all respects only by the end of 26th week. Thus, the path that has the duration of 26 weeks is called the critical path.

Characteristics of Critical Path

(a) A critical path is the longest path (time wise) connecting the initial and final event.

(b) A critical path may run through dummy activities.

(c) The number of activities lying on a critical path may be less than the number of activities in other non-critical paths.

(d) It is possible that the network may have more than one critical path, that is, if two or more paths have the same maximum time duration , then all such paths will have critical paths.

(b) Programme Evaluation and Review Technique (PERT): The critical path method (CPM) uses only one time estimate for each activity, whereas PERT uses three time estimates.

These estimates are used for each activity with the intention of overcoming the uncertainty in project time estimate. The time estimates are given below.

- **Optimistic time estimate**: Under ideal circumstances, it is the shortest time in which an activity can be completed. In arriving at the optimistic time estimate, it is presumed that everything is favourable for completing the activity in the shortest time.

- **Pessimistic time estimate**: It is the maximum time taken to complete an activity under worst circumstances. In arriving at the pessimistic time estimate, it is presumed that everything is unfavourable for completing the activity in time and every possible setback and difficult situation is encountered.

- **Most likely time estimate:** It lies between optimistic and pessimistic time estimates. It is the time in which an activity can be completed under normal situation. In arriving at the most likely time, it is presumed that conditions are neither favourable nor unfavourable, but are normal.

- **Expected time estimate**: PERT assumes that the optimistic time (t_o), the pessimistic time (t_p) will probably occur while the most likely time (t_m) is four times more likely to occur than the other two. Thus, for arriving at the expected time (t_e) equal weights are allotted to t_o and t_p while weight of (t_m) is taken as 4 times that of t_o and t_p.

  Accordingly $t_e = t_o + 4\,t_m + t_p / 6$

  After having arrived at the expected time (t_e) for each activity, the critical path is discovered by making forward pass and backward pass computation, calculating the earliest start time (T_e) and the latest finish time (T_i) of all the events, finding the slack of events and linking the events with zero slack.

3. Graphical Evaluation and Review Technique (GERT)

Graphical evaluation and review technique is the same as PERT, except that it enables numerous project activities by way of looping and branching project activities. Presume that an activity fails because of some unavoidable reasons, and then the project manager has to look for different ways to get the end result.

In the same way, some of the activities may not be performed at all, some may be partly performed and some may be repeated. PERT cannot show alternative plans in a single network diagram and it overcomes these problems as it shows different ways to continue the project.

4. Duration Compression Techniques

When the project manager finds that the expected completion time of the project is more than the desired time he tries to decrease the project time by using compression techniques like crashing, fast tracking etc.

(i) **Crashing:** Here the project manager decreases the project duration by allocating more resources, subcontracting some activities, using more labour etc. The following are the type of activities that are considered for crashing –

(a) A critical activity of the project.

(b) An activity of longer duration.

(c) An activity that has low per unit crash cost.

(d) An activity that does not cause any quantity problems, if crashed.

(e) An activity that is labour intensive.

The crashing procedure is explained below –

(a) Recognise the sequence of activities and prepare a network diagram. Each activity should list the details of normal cost, normal times, crash cost and crash time.

(b) Compare the crashing cost for all project activities using the formula

$$\frac{\text{Crash cost} - \text{Normal cost}}{\text{Normal time} - \text{Crash time}}$$

(c) Rank all the project activities in the ascending order of their crashing cost.

(d) Crash a critical activity that has the least crashing cost, then, calculate the new cost by adding the cost of crashing to the normal cost.

(e) When the critical activity that has the least crashing cost and calculate the new cost by adding the cost of crashing to the normal cost.

(f) When the critical path duration is reduced by crashing, other paths may also become critical. These are called parallel critical paths. So the project duration can be reduced by crashing the activities in the parallel critical paths simultaneously.

(g) The crashing process is continued till further crashing is not possible or it does not result in the reduction of project duration.

(h) For different project durations, the total cost is found. The optimal project duration is found by the project duration corresponding to the minimal total cost.

(ii) **Fast tracking:** In this method the project manager tries to decrease the project duration by doing the project activities separately. Suppose activity B can be started only after the completion of activity A in normal conditions. The project manager can start both activities simultaneously, but makes changes to activity B as per the changes in activity A. This eventually decreases the duration of the complete project.

(iii) Schedule control: Schedule control studies all the factors that have an effect on project schedules. Schedule determines the schedule changes and manages to finish them within the required duration. On the basis of the changes, the project manager updates the project schedule.

The project manager has to consider the project schedule, performance reports and change requests while controlling the schedule. The project schedule represents the planned start and expected finish dates for each project activity.

(iv) Computer Aided Project Management: When the size of the project rises, it becomes difficult and sometimes even impossible to plan, schedule, budget and control activities using manual methods. Thus, with the help of computers the tasks for bigger projects are made simple. It is therefore necessary to have computerised project management system (CPMS) for projects of bigger size and complex nature. The advantages of using CPMS are as under –

(a) CPMS can analyse the problem at very high speed as compared to manual analysis. Due to its high speed, any number of modifications and combinations can be handled easily which cannot be completed manually. For instance, sensitivity analysis of profitability estimate can be completed using computers by altering the different parameters and studying their effect on profit.

(b) Since computers can store and process big volumes of information, CPMS is appropriate for big and complex projects that require handling and analysis of voluminous information.

(c) Accuracy of results produced by CPMS can be depended upon while there is a possibility of committing errors in manual computations.

(d) CPMS improve efficiency and economy of projects as it decreases human resource requirements significantly through clerical and support staff.

(e) Since a project manager who is in direct control of the project can himself directly communicate with the computers and analyse the problem rather than rely on too many of the subordinates, thus can plan correctly and reach best possible decisions.

4.2.4 Cost Dimensions of Project Planning

The structure of financial appraisal stands on correct estimation of the capital cost. If the project cost is under-estimated, the project will have less funds during implementation and there is a risk of the project being stopped if, the promoter is not capable of bringing in additional capital or the financial establishments who has extended project finance is not capable of bringing additional loan to meet the increase in project cost. However, if the project cost is over-estimated, it leads to a situation where more funds are available than necessary and under these situations it is possible that the promoters may divert the resources for other reasons which again is damaging to the interests of both the promoters and the financial establishments.

Components of Capital Cost of a Project

The following are the components that constitute the capital cost of the project:

(a) Land

(b) Land development

(c) Buildings

(d) Plant and machinery

(e) Electricals

(f) Transport and erection charges

(g) Know-how/consultancy fees

(h) Miscellaneous assets

(i) Preliminary and preoperative charges

(j) Provision for contingencies

(k) Margin money for working capital

(a) **Land:** The cost of land includes the legal charges payable for registration of sale deeds.

Before finding the extent of the land and paying the price for such land, the first question to be asked is whether it is important to invest on land and building. If the project is small in size, the likelihood of acquiring a building on lease may be explored. The comparative advantages and effect of profitability between two alternatives, namely starting the project in a leased building and an owned building by obtaining land and constructing building thereon, may be studied. Small projects can be started in leased building which will decrease the cost of the project significantly. It may be noted that only the plant and machinery produces goods and the building only acts as a cover to accommodate the production facilities and the investment in building does not boost the capacity of production. The buildings that are appropriate for the project may not be always available on lease in terms of the size and specifications.

The component 'land' comes into picture only after having decided to buy land and construct building rather than starting the project in a leased premise.

The extent of land should be selected in such a way that it is neither too big as to inflate the cost of the project nor too small to take into consideration possible extensions to the building for near future development.

The extent of land required for a project can be estimated after deciding upon (i) The building plan with adequate allowances for open space around the building (For example, steel foundries and steel rolling stock raw materials in huge quantity in open yards), and (ii) Sufficient provision for expansion in near future, presumably, within a span of three years.

(b) Land development: Land development includes cost of levelling of land, cost of laying internal roads, cost of providing fencing and gates. Land development charges should be carefully evaluated as this is an area where unless carefully planned there is possibility of under estimation.

(c) Buildings: Provision for different types of buildings shall be predicted and provided for. The following are the types of buildings that are to be provided for any project:

- Main factory building
- Ancillary factory building
- Administrative buildings
- Laboratory
- Godowns
- Toilet blocks
- Overhead/underground water storage tanks
- Canteen, rest rooms, guesthouses
- Quarters for essential staff etc.

The plant layout appropriate for the proposed project should be studied and analysed. The size of the main factory building depends upon the plant layout. It must be guaranteed that the built-up area of different buildings proposed is enough to meet the needs and no unnecessary construction is completed. The type of roof a building has plays an important role in determining the cost of a building. Offices are usually constructed with reinforced concrete slab roofing as this gives a dust and sound proof environment and is also appropriate for air-conditioning of rooms. The factory hall, godowns and other buildings are generally given industrial roofing, which may be a combination of steel/concrete trusses and ACC sheet/GI sheet roofing sheets. The height of factory building should also be properly decided after considering the height of machinery proposed to be erected, the headroom needed for operating the plant and machinery, the requirements of overhead cranes if any etc. After attaining the size and design of different buildings, their cost of construction can be reached by preparing a comprehensive estimate and assigning the work to a qualified civil/structural engineer.

(d) Plant and machinery: Indigenous plants: Cost of indigenous plants includes basic price as well as sales tax, octroi and other taxes, if any.

While selecting machinery suppliers and to have their actual information, their reputation and past performance, and the performance of machinery that was supplied before is to be studied. The quotations from a few reputed machinery suppliers can be acquired and comparative study of the prices quoted by them are required to be studied before determining upon the supplier and the relevant machinery. Except for the price other factors like the market reputation of the supplier, the differences in machinery specifications of different suppliers, their service network to effect after sales-service are also to be taken into consideration and these factors are to be correctly weighed before reaching a decision.

Imported plants: The cost of imported plant and machinery is the landed cost, that is, Free-on-Board (FOB) value of the plant + freight charges + insurance + import duty + clearing, loading and unloading charges etc. It is sensible to import the required spare parts along with the imported plant. In case of import of second hand machinery due care should be implemented about the price and quality of the machine particularly the working condition and the evaluation of unexpired future life. One should take the assistance of an independent skilled engineer after checking the machinery.

(e) Electricals: The costs of electrical items consist of the cost of cables, panel boards, voltage stabilisers etc. Whenever the industry is to attract power from a high tension power line, necessary voltage step-down transformers should be included in the project and its cost should be accounted for.

(f) Transport and Erection Charges: Transportation charges till the plant and machinery reaches the factory site, including loading and unloading charges to be accounted for, erection charges comprise of machinery foundation cost and machinery assembling and erection expenses.

(g) Know-how/Consultancy Fees: The following are the expenses that are included under the head -

  (i) Know-how fees to technical consultants.

  (ii) Expenses of training employees in the production process.

(h) Miscellaneous assets: These are the assets that are associated with industrial activity, but are not a part of the plant and machinery. For instance, office tools, furniture, fire fighting tools, water coolers, air conditioners etc. come under this group. These assets, though not a part of industrial equipments, are to be incorporated in the project and adequately provided for in the project cost. Cash deposits with electricity boards for getting power connection, advances made to lesser while leasing the building etc. which are in the nature of refundable deposits are incorporated under this head.

(i) Preliminary and preoperative expenses: These are the expenses that are incurred before the project takes shape and starts commercial production. The following expenses come under this head.

  • Investigation fee, service charges etc. to banks/financial institutions.

  • Commitment charges payable on loan offered by banks/financial institutions.

If the project promoters do not draw the loan as per commitment given to financial establishments for drawing loans, in different phases, the bank/financial establishments charges commitment charges on the amount and the period not drawn, since the bank/financial institution has to maintain adequate amount of liquid cash to meet the loan disbursements as and when planned.

- Interest on term loans during implementation period.

Banks/Financial establishments offer holiday period for repaying the principal loan amount. The moratorium for the repayment of principal loan amount will depend on the project implementation schedule and is usually set in such a way that the first instalment of term loan repayment begins after allowing reasonable period beyond the date of commencement of commercial production. On the other hand, interest on term loan is to be paid right from the date of disbursement of term loan. If a project has drawn loan in phases during a specific period of time, interest on the term loan amount is payable in periodical or half yearly instalments as determined by the financial establishments.

- Mortgage expenses
- Expenses on capital issues
- Other miscellaneous expenses during the project implementation stage
- Insurance charges

Both fixed assets and current assets (inventory) are to be insured against possible damage by the accident. Banks and financial institutions insist that the assets financed by them be insured, assets are insured as and when they are created.

(j) Provision for Contingencies: The cost estimates of land, land development, building, plant and machinery, electrical, transport and erection etc. that are based on specific assumptions. While implementing the project, the actual cost may be at variance with the estimate because of the following – (a) the price of plant and machinery may arise, the sales tax, excise duty etc. may get revised on the higher side; (b) in the case of imported plant and machinery, the cost in terms of rupee may rise because of bad fluctuations in foreign exchange rates and (c) during implementing the project there may be minor deviations needed to suit the field conditions – some equipments which were not originally foreseen may be needed to be incorporated etc.

In order to meet such unexpected but unavoidable rise in costs, there must be provision in the project cost. This is done by making a contingency provision in the project cost which may differ from 5 percent to 15 percent of the cost of non-firm items. A higher contingency provision is needed if the implementation period is longer as there are chances of increase in cost with the passage of time.

(k) Margin money for working capital: Any project requires funds on two accounts – first, for establishing the project which includes investments on fixed assets and secondly for maintaining the operations of the plant which includes investment on working capital. Banks/financial establishments extend term loans for investment on fixed assets while financing of working capital requirement is completed mostly by banks. In both the type of financing (fixed assets and working capital) the financier expects a margin to be brought in by the promoters. The complete requirement is not financed by way of loan. If the total working capital requirement is ₹ 50 lakhs and if the banks that finance the working capital requirements specifies a margin requirement of 25 percent, the promoters need to bring in ₹ 12.50 lakhs toward the share of working capital and the remaining ₹ 37.50 lakhs (75 percent) will be brought by the banks/financial establishments. The share of promoters' contribution towards the working capital is integrated as a part of project cost. And since it is financed through long-term sources of financing, it is included in the project cost.

Cost Control Techniques

Following are some of the valuable and important techniques used for efficient project cost control.

1. **Planning the Project Budget:** One is ideally required to make a budget at the start of the planning session regarding the project at hand. It is this budget that would help one for all payments that is required to be made and costs that one will incur during the project lifecycle. The making of this budget thus entails a lot of research and critical thinking.

   Like any other budget, one should leave room for adjustments as the costs may not remain the same right through the period of the project. Following the project budget at all times is the key to the profit from project.

2. **Keeping a Track of Costs:** Keeping track of all actual costs is also just as significant as any other method. Here, it is best to prepare a budget that is based on time. This will help one keep track of the budget of a project in each of its stages. The actual costs will have to be tracked against the periodic targets that have been used in the budget. These targets could be on a monthly, weekly or even yearly basis if the project will continue for long.

   This is much simple to work with rather than having one complete budget for the complete period of the project. If any new work is needed to be performed, one is required to make estimations for this and see if it can be accommodated with the final amount in the budget. If not, one may have to work on necessary arrangements for 'change requests', where the customer will pay for the new changes.

3. **Effective Time Management:** Another effective technique is effective time management. Even though this technique is applied to different management areas, it is very important regarding project cost control.

The reason for this is that the cost of one's project could keep increasing if one is not capable of meeting the project deadlines; the longer the project is prolonged, the higher the costs incurred which effectively means that the budget will be exceeded.

The project manager would need to continuously remind his/her team of the significant deadlines of the project so as to guarantee that the work is finished on time.

4. **Project Change Control:** Project change control is yet another important technique. Change control systems are important to consider any potential changes that could occur during the course of the project.

   This is because of the fact that each change to the scope of the project will affect the deadlines of the deliverables, so the changes might increase the project cost by increasing the effort required for the project.

5. **Use of Earned Value:** In the same way, in order to recognise the value of the work that has been performed thus far, it is very helpful to use the accounting technique generally known as 'Earned Value'.

   This is especially helpful for big projects and will help one make any quick changes that are extremely important for the project to be successful.

Order of Magnitude Estimate

We have seen the method of arriving at the project cost by estimating the cost of individual components of the project. At the preliminary stage of project formulation, a project promoter may like to know about the estimated cost of the project that he wants to carry out. Only after understanding the estimated cost of the project that he has in mind, he can go for further detailed study. There are some techniques available that are helpful in estimating the possible cost of a proposed project. These techniques of estimating the project cost identified by the term 'order of magnitude estimate' are very rough, but quick estimates. The following are some of the techniques used for arriving at a rough estimate of project cost.

(a) **Investment per unit of output:** The investment pattern of similar projects is compared with the proposed project. For instance, if the likely investment on a project for establishing a cement plant is needed to be estimated, the investment made on an existing cement plant is taken as a reference.

Let, I_e = Investment made on an existing project

         C_e = Installed capacity of the existing project

         I_p = Investment required for the proposed project

         C_p = Installed capacity of the proposed project

Then, $I_p = I_e/C_e \times C_p$

(b) Turnover Ratio: This technique takes the ratio of sales turnover to investment as the reference.

Let,

T_e = Turnover achieved by an existing project

T_p = Turnover of the proposed project

I_e = Investment made on the existing project

I_p = Investment required for the proposed project

Then, $I_p = I_e/T_e \times T$

(c) Inflation Index: The technique compares the investment made on a similar project with the same capacity as that of the proposed project. The investment made on an existing project of similar nature and capacity is taken as reference and this investment is corrected for the inflation that has occurred during the time gap of investment on the two projects.

Let,

I_e = Investment made on an existing project

I_p = Investment required for the proposed project

Then,

$I_p = I_e \times$ consumer price index (present) / consumer price index at the time of investment on the project that is taken as reference

(d) Location Index: When similar projects are not available within the country for comparison, similar projects executed overseas can be taken as reference for reaching a tentative estimate of the cost of the proposed project. The tentative estimate of project cost arrived at may be corrected by implementing appropriate correction factors to account for the difference in cost of material and labour between the two projects.

Estimating Costs

For practical reasons, cost estimates are frequently made at a level of aggregation that includes many work packages. The resources that are used on individual work packages are controlled in terms of physical quantities, rather than cost and costing out each work package would serve of no valuable purpose.

Preparing the Control Budget

The control budget is prepared close to the inception of the work, allowing just enough time for approval by decision makers prior to the commitment of costs. For a long duration project, the initial control budget may be prepared in detail only for the first phase of the project, with fairly rough cost estimates for later phases. Detailed budgets for the later phases are prepared just before starting the work on these phases. Delaying preparation of the control budget until just before beginning the work guarantees that the control budget includes existing information about scope and schedule, the result of cost analyses, and current data about wage rates, material prices, and other variables. Therefore it avoids making budget estimates that are based on outdated information.

4.2.5 Quality Dimensions of Project Planning

Quality planning plays an important role in various business processes. Each organisation defines their view of quality in terms that deliver the greatest alignment with their unique business values. For this reason, it is difficult to create a single definition of quality that covers every aspect of every organisation. Thus, it is more suitable to discuss the framework of quality planning by dividing the subject into two particular parts – quality policy and quality objectives.

Project quality management is a difficult area to define. Its main purpose is to guarantee that the project will fulfil the requirements for which it was carried out. To achieve this, the project team must develop good relations with key stakeholders and know what quality means to them. It is through this association that quality will be defined. Many technical projects do not succeed because the project team concentrates only on meeting the written requirements for the products that were mentioned originally and neglecting other stakeholder requirements and expectations. For instance, the project team should know the importance of the customer's terms if the item is delivered as specified. On the basis of the viewpoints outlined here, quality must be on an equal level of importance with project scope, time, and cost.

Any organisation that is serious about success must define its quality goals to be in line with their customers' requirements and the strategic goals of the organisation. These goals are categorised into a set of standard quality requirements that are an essential part, perhaps even the end goal of the project quality plan.

Quality Dimensions Criteria

Quality as defined from the consumers' viewpoint has less defects and several features that meet the consumer's requirements. These two aspects are the cornerstone for an effective quality assurance program. The key, according to David Garvin is not just in defending consumers from annoyances but also in satisfying them (**Garvin, 1987**). The following are eight dimensions of quality as defined by David Garvin along with the interpretation of how that quality can be used within a custom home construction project.

- **Performance** refers to the product's overall working features with measurable attributes. Performance of the project can be calculated through the timeliness of the project schedule and the proximity of the project to the budget.

- **Features** are the secondary facets of a product's basic functions. The features of the project would also be the timeliness with which the firm will be a custom home project together with the additional construction aspects of our custom design.

- **Reliability** refers to the possibility of a product malfunctioning. Reliability within the project would be found in one's capability to maintain schedule and stay on budget.

- **Conformance** is the design and feature of a product that meets established standards as it applies to defect rates and number of complaints or calls for service from consumers. Conformance within a project would be the established and historical craftsmanship of the firm's custom homes.

- **Durability** is the amount of times a product is used before it wears down. Durability within a project is found in the quality of craftsmanship and the absence of homeowner maintenance after 5 and 10 years of possession.

- **Serviceability** is the consumer's capability to receive speed, courtesy, competence and ease of repair. Serviceability within a project is found in the relationship set up with the homeowner and adjusting to their personal need or desires for the project.

- **Aesthetics** are the look, feel, taste, smell and sound of a product. Aesthetics within a project are the custom hardwood cabinets in every wet area, rounded corners, granite on all countertops and more.

- **Perceived quality** is the reputation and other indirect measures that are the basis for a consumer to select one product over another. Perceived quality within a project is a history of building a fine custom home at a reasonable price in a swift timeframe.

To end with, quality begins with a communication of an organisational culture that establishes the vision, policies and goals for maintaining said quality. The culture of an organisation must start and remain with quality as the first priority. A firm has made a name for itself as a firm that does a job right the first time and without excuses.

Quality Dimensions	Description of what it is in terms of project	Criteria to measure	Meets or exceeds criteria
Performance	Whether the project is on time and budget.	Assess MS Project timelines and budget flows.	
Features	The custom design aspects of the custom home.	Make sure design is outside of spec home deliverables.	

contd. ...

Reliability	Refers to the quality of the craftsmanship and also the ability to stay on time and budget for the project.	Using only the best materials and qualified craftsmen to build the home.	
Conforms	Conformance is the historical reputation of ABC construction company.	Make sure all bonding issues are settled before contracting and before start date of project.	
Durability	Points to the lack of homeowner maintenance required for the first 5 and 10 years of ownership.	By using only the most qualified and following a historically accurate plan.	
Serviceability	Homeowner has initial autonomy and chooses several custom aspects of the construction and design.	Allowing homeowners to be in on all project stakeholder meetings and listening and adhering to their requests.	
Aesthetics	Custom aspects like hardwood in high areas and tiles in all wet areas as well as customs cabinets throughout the home.	No cutting of corners here. Only the best craftsmanship and quality materials for the project.	
Perception	The reputation of quality custom home building precedes ABC construction company.	Doing a job right the first time, every time is how to build a positive perception.	

Implications for Project Planning Stage

The feedback from previous projects can add insight on quality that can be attainable. Planning involves recognising the products (deliverables) at the beginning of the project and deciding the best steps to verify and validate them so that they meet the standards. Applying resources toward output monitoring during each stage will help us recognise the problems faster.

Project quality and deliverable quality are two different aspects of focus. Project quality refers to following the correct project management practices and adhering to the company objectives whereas deliverable quality refers to the correct product or deliverables that meets user's requirements. A high project quality may have low deliverable quality and high deliverable quality may have low project quality. The PM must manage both aspects of the effort.

The PM and his quality team must be aware of the existing quality policy level of the firm and assess whether this level is suitable in meeting the quality level specified by the customer. If there is any uncertainty of meeting customer expectations, then the project management team must know about this and take steps toward improving the existing quality approach. This may require creating new processes or demand more resources or tools to improve the quality level. Embedded in this decision process are the associated cost and schedule impacts related to the quality level (cost of quality). An appropriate balance between quality and other performance variables needs to be carefully analysed and communicated with senior management and the customer. From this, a formal agreement should be documented as trade-offs in some dimension are frequently required.

Project quality management processes help prevent recurring problems by organising and managing resources to ensure that project deliverables are completed on time, within budget, and are of high user-perceived quality.

The main tenets of project quality management are as follows:

- **Customer satisfaction:** Customer satisfaction requires the understanding, evaluation, definition, and management of expectations so that suitable requirements are established.
- **Prevention inspection:** Prevention over inspection is the commonsense principle meaning that the cost of preventing mistakes is usually much less than the cost of correcting them.
- **Management responsibility:** Management's responsibility in quality management is to provide the resources required to sustain success and protect the project team front environmental disruption.
- **Continuous improvement:** Continuous improvement basically involves following the plan-do-check-act (PDCA) cycle of quality improvement.

4.3 Project Control

4.3.1 Introduction

Project controls is a function and any one person may fulfil parts or all of the function as defined and incorporate other allied function such as different aspects of contract and project administration within their specific job description.

There are several definitions of project controls used across industries and firms within industries. For the purposes of this portal, the field of project controls is defined as follows.

Project controls are the data gathering, management and analytical processes used to forecast, understand and influence the time and cost outcomes of a project or program; through communicating the information in formats that help effective management and decision-making. This definition includes all stages of a project or program's lifecycle from the initial estimating required to 'size' a proposed project, through reflective learning and the forensic analysis required to understand the reasons for failure.

Project control has to be exercised on two accounts.

(i) During the execution phase and

(ii) Project evaluation after the project is completed

4.3.2 Role of Project Control

Consequently, the project controls discipline can be seen as encompassing:

- Project strategy, undertaking planning and methods studies to assist the PM optimise future results;
- Scheduling including development, updating and maintenance;
- Cost estimation, cost engineering/control and value engineering;
- Risk management, including maintaining the risk register and risk analysis/ evaluation;
- Earned value management and earned schedule, including WBS, OBS and other breakdown structures;
- Document control;
- Forensic assessment for required diagnosis of schedule and cost.
- Supplier performance measurement/oversight (but excluding contract administration);
- The elements of a project management methodology that integrate these disciplines both within the 'controls' domain and with other project management functions;
- Stakeholder analytics and issues tracking but excluding stakeholder engagement and management;

- Some statistical aspects of quality control as they have an effect on future performance and the prediction of project results; as well as any aspects quality directly connected to the management and performance of the project controls function itself such as measuring the quality of the information used for estimation.

- Potential elements of organisational governance, culture and ethics as they apply to project and program teams and have an effect on their work;

- Developing, maintaining and using relevant historical data sets (lessons learned/ production rates/knowledge management etc.); and

- The ability to effectively communicate the information to the management that is generated by these processes.

Altogether, project controls encompass the people, processes and tools used to plan, manage and mitigate cost and schedule issues and any risk events that may have an effect on a project. In other words, project control is basically the same as the project management process deprived of its facilitating sub-processes for safety, quality, organisational, behavioural, and communications management.

4.3.3 Difference in Management Control of Projects with Management Control of Ongoing Operations

The control system in a project is different from ongoing operations. At times, when a project is completed it leads to an ongoing operation, as in the case of a successful development project. The change from the project organisation to the operating organisation involves complex management control issues. Different features of projects that make the management control different regarding ongoing operations are discussed below.

(i) **Single objective:** A project generally has a single objective whereas ongoing operations have numerous objectives. Besides supervising daily work, the manager of a responsibility centre in an ongoing organisation must both manage existing job and also make decisions that have an effect on future operations. Although the project manager also makes decisions that have an effect on the future, the time horizon is the end of the project.

(ii) **Organisation structure:** In several cases, the project organisation is superimposed on an ongoing operating organisation and its management control system is superimposed on the management control system of that organisation.

(iii) **Focus on the project:** Project control focuses on the project, whose goals are to produce a satisfactory product within a particular time period and at a best possible cost. On the contrary, control in ongoing organisation focuses on the activities of a specified time period, such as a month, and on all the products worked on in that period.

(iv) Need for trade-offs: Projects usually involve trade-offs between scope, schedule and cost. Similar trade-offs take place in ongoing organisations, but they are not typical of the daily activities in such organisation.

(v) Less reliable standards: Performance standards are likely to be less reliable for projects than for ongoing organisations.

(vi) Frequent changes in plans: Plans for projects are changed often and significantly because of unpredicted environmental conditions revealed during a consulting engagement.

(vii) Different rhythm: The rhythm of a project varies from that of ongoing operations. Most projects begin small, rise to a peak activity and then diminish as completion nears. Ongoing activities have a tendency to function at a same level for a significant time and then change.

(viii) Greater environmental influence: Projects are influenced more by the external environment than is the case with operations in a factory.

(ix) Information structure: In a project control system, the smallest element is called a "work package" and these work packages are aggregated to "work breakdown structure", for example, work package – electrical work. Each work package should be the responsibility of a single manager.

Besides work packages, estimated costs for administrative and support activities are stated as per unit of time, just as overhead costs of ongoing responsibility centre.

Due to the above varying features, management control of projects is different from management control of ongoing operations. The most significant difference is that the ongoing operations continue forever whereas a project ends. Fig. 4.3 shows this part. The elements in the management control of operations reappear, one leads to the next in a prescribed way and time. Although some operating activities change from one month to the next, many of them continue to be the same, month after month, or even year after year. By contrast, a project begins, moves forward from one milestone to the next and then stops. During its life, plans are made at regular intervals and these may cause a modification in the plan.

A - In an Operating Organisation

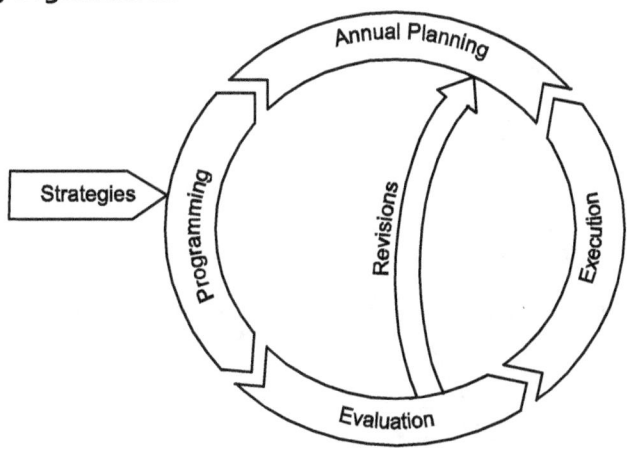

The Control Environment

B - In a Project

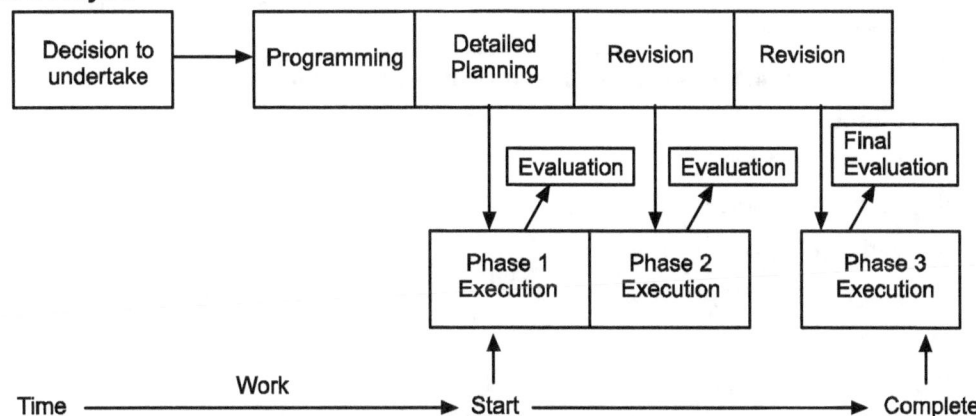

Fig. 4.3: Phases of Management Control

4.3.4 Project Execution

At the final stage of the planning process, for most projects there is a specification of work packages, a schedule, and a budget; also, the manager who is accountable for each work package is recognised. The schedule shows the estimated time for each activity, and the budget shows estimated costs of each major part of the project. This information is frequently stated in a financial model. The resources to be used in complete work packages are communicated in non-monetary terms such as the number of person-days needed, the control budget states monetary costs only for a sizable aggregation of individual work packages. In the control process, information on actual cost, time and accomplishment are compared with these estimates. The comparison may be made either when an assigned milestone in the project is arrived at or at specified time intervals, such as weekly or monthly.

4.3.5 Control Reports

The management information system must be developed to generate the required reports so that cost, time and work can be observed. Different levels of management need different reports at differing frequencies. Fig. 4.4 gives a pictorial idea about report requirements at different levels.

There are several reports and information that are required regularly as well as on a need basis. A list of three types of reports is given below.

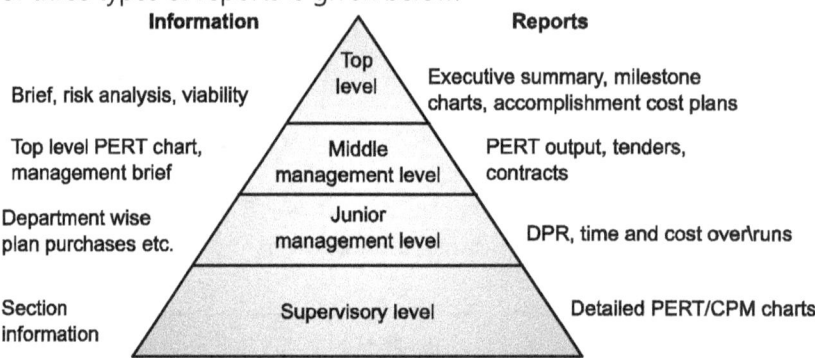

Fig. 4.4: Management levels and required information

1. **Cost Reports**
    (a) Activity cost report
    (b) Cost flow report
    (c) Variance report

2. **Time and Effort Reports**
    (a) Time activity report
    (b) Time analysis report
        • Programme schedule and work efforts are inter-related.
        • These reports provide PERT/CPM type information.

3. **Work Status Report**
        • Status index report (this report tries to merge all three – cost, time and work into a single index)

Alternatively, the types of reports can be listed in six parts as follows.

1. **Financial Reports**
    (a) Monthly commitment and expenditure.
    (b) Monthly cash flow forecast.
    (c) Monthly bank guarantee position.
    (d) Monthly outstanding payments to consultants, suppliers, and contractors.
    (e) Weekly retirement of documents through bank.

2. **Procurement-Monthly Reports**

    (a) Orders placement details.

    (b) Pending orders schedule.

    (c) Bids processing status.

    (d) Delivery forecast.

3. **Inspection Expediting Reports**

    (a) Weekly vendor-wise details status report.

    (b) Constraints report – technical and commercial.

    (c) Exception report.

    (d) Sub-ordering report.

4. **Engineering Reports**

    (a) Documents release and balance status report (monthly).

    (b) Bid's technical scrutiny and recommendation report.

    (c) Construction drawings – release and status report.

    (d) Operation manual.

    (e) Model.

5. **Construction and Erection Report**

    (a) Weekly job-wise, contractor-wise report.

    (b) Monthly detailed progress review.

    (c) Exception report.

6. **Project Management**

    (a) Monthly overall review covering above aspects.

    (b) Exceptions and recommendations.

The frequency and the details of project control reports are very need specific and so will differ from company to company and from project to project. Some general points concerning the reports are summarised below.

4.3.6 Reports on Cost and Time

Reports on actual cost compared to budget and actual time compared to the schedule are comparatively simple. The interpretation of the time reports is comparatively simple.

In interpreting the time reports, the common assumption is that if a work package is finished in less than the estimated time, the responsible supervisor is to be applauded, but if more than the estimated time has been spent, questions are raised. The interpretation of the cost reports is a bit different, for the likelihood exists that if the actual costs are less than the budget, quality may have suffered. For this reason, unless there is some independent way of estimating what costs should have been; good cost performance is frequently interpreted as meaning being on budget, neither higher nor lower.

Inputs

The inputs to cost control are the cost baseline, performance reports, change requests and the cost management plan.

The cost baseline is the output from the cost budgeting process explained before. Performance reports which are a part of performance reporting deal with reporting and feedback and give information on a project's cost performance and attract attention towards activities and work packages that are not meeting their to-date targets.

All facets of change need to be summarised within a change control procedure; an important input to such a process will be the cost change requests that will probably affect the varying budget.

The cost management plan – one of the outputs from the cost estimating process is again part of the overall project management plan and deals with how the cost variances are to be managed.

Tools and Techniques

The tools and techniques of cost control are the cost change control system, performance measurement, additional planning and necessary computerised tools.

The cost change control system will establish the procedures by which the cost baseline may be altered. Certainly, this aspect of control is only a part of the overall chance control that is required for managing the projects.

Performance management, using such methods as complete percentage of each activity, earned value analysis etc. assists in the project scam's evaluation of the health or status of a project at any time. Earned value, compares the amount of work that was planned with what was actually achieved, to decide if progress is as planned.

Outputs

The anticipated outputs from cost control are:

- Revised cost estimates
- Budget updates
- Corrective action
- Estimate at completion
- Lessons learned

In other words, changes made to generate the cost estimates may be the result of experiences gained from the cost control process. From the performance measurement and change control system, any and all changes that would create cost variances are organised and the budget updated.

Corrective action is all the work required to bring the future performance of the project at the level of the project plan.

Forecasting the estimate refers to the need to decide the final project at any time during partial completion. All reasons for cost variances experienced, and the corrective action executed, need to be recorded and used as lessons learned in all future projects.

4.3.7 Reports on Output-Revisions

If a project is complex or if it is of longer duration, it is possible that the plan may not be followed in one or more of its three aspects – scope, schedule, or cost. A common incidence is that there is likely to be a cost overrun, that is, actual costs will surpass the budgeted costs. If this occurs, the sponsor can take any of the three options.

(i)   Accept the over-run and proceed with the project as originally planned.

(ii) Decide to cut back on the scope of the project, with the aim of producing an end product that is within the original cost limitation or

(iii) Decide to substitute the project manager if the sponsor concludes that the budget over-run was unnecessary. Whatever the decision, it generally leads to a revised plan. In some cases, the sponsor may judge that the current estimate of benefits is lower than the current cost-to-complete estimate and thus decide to end the project.

If the plan is revised there is subsequent comparison of actual with both the original plan and the revised plan. The following example shows the report in two parts. The first part shows the original plan, the revisions that have been authorised so far and the reasons for making them. Another segment shows the revised budget and the current estimate of costs.

Original budget	₹ 1000
Authorised revisions to date	
For inflation	50
For specification changes	200
For time delays	60
For cost savings	30
Revised budget	1280
Current estimate to complete	1400
Variance	120
Explanation of variance	
Material cost variance	20
Overtime	60
Spending variance	40
	120

Project Auditing

In several projects the audit of quality is completed on time. If it is postponed, the defective work on individual work packages may be concealed, if they are covered up by the following work. For example, the quality of plumbing work on a construction project cannot be verified after walls and ceilings have been completed.

As the work progresses, projects audit of costs are also completed, in others the cost audit is not prepared until the project is finished.

Recently, internal auditors have extended their function into what is known as operational auditing. Besides examining the costs incurred, they reveal management actions that they believe are unsatisfactory. The operational auditing that is completed correctly can be of use. The auditors should predict the actions that the managers have taken considering the situation prevailing at the time decisions are taken.

4.3.8 Project Evaluation

The evaluation and control of projects has two separate aspects.

1. An evaluation of performance in implementing the project and
2. An evaluation of the results obtained from the project.

The former is performed soon after the project has been finished; the latter may not be possible until many years later.

Evaluation of Performance

The evaluation of performance in executing the project has two aspects.

1. **An evaluation of project management:** The purpose is to help in decisions concerning project managers, including rewards, promotions, constructive criticisms, or reassignment.

2. **An evaluation of the process of managing the project:** To find out better ways of carrying out future projects. In several cases these evaluations are informal.

If the results of the project were unsatisfactory and if the project was significant, a formal evaluation is useful. Also, formal evaluation of a successful project or of a significant unsatisfactory project may recognise methods that will improve performance on future projects.

Because work on a project is less standardised and vulnerable to measurement than work in a factory, evaluation of a project is more subjective than assessment of production activities. It looks like the assessment of marketing activities in that appraisal of performance requires that the effect of external factors on performance be considered.

In looking back at how well the work on the project was managed, the natural temptation is to depend on information that was not available at the time. In retrospect, one can generally find out about those cases in which the "right" decision was not made. On the other hand, the decision made at the time may have been completely reasonable; the manager may not have had all the information at that time; or the manager may not have addressed a specific problem because other problems had a higher priority; or the manager may have based the decision on personality considerations, trade-offs, or other factors that are not documented in written reports.

However, some positive signs of poor management may be recognised. Diversion of funds or other assets that is personally useful to the project manager is a clear example. If there were major specification changes or cost overruns, these changes should have been sanctioned, and cash flows should have been recalculated in order to decide whether the return on the project was still acceptable. Still another example of poor management is a manager's failure to tighten a control system that allows others to steal, but this is harder to judge because overly tight controls may hinder progress on the project. Evidence that the manager regards cost control as much insignificant as an excellent finished product finished on schedule, is another sign of poor management, but it is not conclusive. The sponsor may overlook budget over-runs if the product is excellent, as it frequently happens for motion picture projects.

The assessment of the process may show that reviews conducted during the project were inadequate, or based on these reviews a timely action was not taken. For example, the review may show that based on the information available at the time, the project should have been redirected or even stopped, but this was not completed. This may suggest that more often or thorough analysis, progress should have been made; as a result, requirements for such reviews on future projects should be altered.

The assessment may also bring about changes in rules or procedure. It may recognise some rules that needlessly hindered efficient conduct of the project. On the other hand, it may expose inadequate controls. As part of the evaluation, suggestions for improving the process should be solicited from project employees.

Evaluation of Results

The success of a project cannot be evaluated until sufficient time has elapsed to allow measurement of its actual benefits and costs. This may take years. Unless the effect can be particularly measured, such an evaluation may not be useful. For example, the benefits of installing a labour saving machine will not be identifiable, if the resulting costs are buried in several product costs and not separately traced to the new machine. Moreover, there is no point in trying to assess a project unless some action can be taken on the basis of this analysis.

For several projects, evaluation of results is complicated by the fact that the expected benefits were not stated in objective, measurable terms, and the actual benefits also were not measurable.

Points to Remember

- A **project** is a set of activities meant to achieve a specified end result of sufficient significance to be of interest to the management of an organisation.

- **Project planning** defines the project activities and end products that will be carried out and describe how the activities can be completed.

- The three constraints in a project management triangle are time, cost and scope.

- **Scheduling** is nothing but the arrangement of activities of the project in the order of time in which they are to be performed.

- A **bar chart** is a pictorial representation indicating the different activities that are involved in a project.

- **Quality** as defined from the consumers' viewpoint has less defects and several features that meet the consumer's requirements.

- **Project controls** is a function and any one person may fulfil parts or all of the function as defined and incorporate other allied function such as different aspects of contract and project administration within their specific job description.

- In interpreting the time reports, the common assumption is that if a work package is finished in less than the estimated time, the responsible supervisor is to be applauded, but if more than the estimated time has been spent, questions are raised. The interpretation of the cost reports is a bit different, for the likelihood exists that if the actual costs are less than the budget, quality may have suffered.

- If the plan is revised there is subsequent comparison of actual with both the original plan and the revised plan.

Questions for Discussion

1. Point out the difference in management control of projects with management control of ongoing operations.

2. How will you plan the time and cost dimensions in project management?

3. Explain in detail the three dimensional structure of a project control system.

4. Describe the control environment of a project.

5. Write short notes on:

    (i)   Nature of the Project Plan

    (ii)   Network Analysis

    (iii) Network Based Scheduling

    (iv) Critical Path Method

    (v)   Graphical Evaluation and Review Technique (GERT)

    (vi) Duration Compression Techniques

6. What do you know about computer-aided project management, essential requirements of project management software?

7. Can you describe the project planning and performance evaluation techniques in respect of a project?

■■■

Chapter **5**...

Implementing MCS for Small and Medium Size Companies

Contents ...

5.4   Management Control System in a Non-Profit Organisation

    5.4.1   Non-Profit Organisations

    5.4.2   Profit-Oriented Corporations vs. Non-Profit Organisations

    5.4.3   Distinctive Characteristics of Non-Profit Organisations

    5.4.4   Issues Involved in Drafting Management Control System in a Non-Profit Organisation

    • Points to Remember

    • Questions for Discussion

Learning Objectives ...

- To understand the management control system for small and medium enterprises
- To explain the methodology of implementing management control systems
- To discuss the tools and techniques for implementing management control systems
- To gain knowledge on management control structure
- To explain the types of responsibility centres
  - (a) Cost Centres
  - (b) Revenue Centres
  - (c) Profit Centres
  - (d) Investment Centres
- To discuss the management control systems of service organisations
- To explain the management control system in a non-profit organisation

5.1 Management Control System for Small and Medium Enterprises

5.1.1 Introduction

There is no certainty that management control systems will always be successful, either in terms of design or implementation. These systems can only raise the probability of attaining organisational objectives of effectiveness, efficiency, accuracy of financial reporting, and compliance.

Management controls should be incorporated into the organisation's activities. These in-built control systems will control the organisation's ability to attain its objectives and also assist in improving the quality of its business operations. There are five components of management control – control environment, risk assessment, control activities, information and communication, and monitoring the control system.

Control activities relate to the policies and processes that are used in an organisation to give a guarantee that the directions and instructions given by the management are followed properly.

Control activities vary depending on the business setting, organisational goals, and difficulty in business operations, the people involved in the execution of these activities, and organisational structure and culture. Conducting meetings assists in improving decision-making and also in decreasing the time taken for the decision-making process. There are four different types of meetings which serve different purposes and they are the daily check-in, the weekly tactical, the monthly strategic, and the quarterly off-site review.

Information systems will not be useful without appropriate communication between the different levels of management. Communication is not only needed to forward the information but is also necessary for co-ordinating work, allotting responsibilities, etc. Two types of communications – internal communication and external communication – take place in any organisation.

The management controls are designed in such a way that the control activities involved are checked on a constant basis or separately. Continuous monitoring assists the organisation by providing feedback on whether the control components are effective or ineffective. Separate evaluation of activities assists in knowing about the effectiveness of the control system in total and, in turn, of the continuous monitoring processes. The most significant factor while executing control systems is that the organisations should have correct procedures in position to recognise, communicate, follow up, and rectify discrepancies in the plans and objectives that are fixed.

Management control is executed by numerous people both internal and external to the organisation. Each of them plays a different role and has different responsibilities toward the effective operation of a management control system. The entities that are inside the organisation are the management, board of directors, internal auditors, and employees; the entities external to the organisation consist of external auditors, regulatory bodies, customers, suppliers, and financial analysts.

Control is a process that is implemented by individuals, and the related processes should be practiced attentively, instead of practising it mechanically. Consistency of implementation is another key requirement for the administration of management control systems in an organisation, to be successful. The issues faced in execution can be those which delay the management control process or dysfunctional results of executing the management control system.

Some issues that delay management control process are absence of good organisational structure, management style, well-defined hierarchy, etc. lack of good person-job and person-reward fit; deficiencies in training and developing employees; conspiracy between the controlled person and the controlling person; illegal use of management power; and absence of good communication.

The execution and administration of management control systems can cause dysfunctional effects that are counterproductive to the attainment of organisational goals. It is necessary to personally observe the control system to see whether it is really encouraging managers and employees to act for the sake of the organisation, so that necessary corrective actions may be taken during implementation. Some dysfunctional results of management control systems are excessive quantification and effort to determine all possible measures, presence of standard operating procedures limiting innovation, and data management.

5.1.2 Small and Medium Enterprises in India

In India small and medium enterprises (SME) is a general word used to describe small scale industrial (SSI) units and medium-scale industrial units. An industrial unit with a total investment in its fixed assets or leased assets or hire-purchase assets up to ₹ 10 million is regarded as a SSI unit, and investment up to ₹ 100 million is regarded as a medium unit. Besides that, an SSI unit can neither be a subsidiary nor can it be possessed or controlled by any other industrial unit. The SME sector generates a broad range of industrial products like food products, beverages, tobacco and tobacco products, cotton textiles, wool, silk, synthetic products, jute, hemp and jute products, wood and wood products, furniture and fixtures, paper and paper products, printing, publishing and allied industries, machinery, machines, apparatus, appliances and electrical machinery. SME sector also has several big service industries.

The small scale sector in India includes different variety of units from traditional crafts to high-tech industries. There are about twenty-one chief industry groups in the small scale sector that include food products, chemical and chemical products, basic metal industries, metal products, electrical machinery and parts, rubber and plastic products, machinery and parts except electrical goods, hosiery and garments, wood products, non-metallic mineral products, paper products and printing, transport equipments and parts, leather and leather products, manufacturing industries, other services and

- Microwave components
- Plastic film capacitors
- Carbon film registers
- Electro medical equipments
- Electronic teaching aids
- Digital measuring equipments
- Air-conditioning equipments
- Optical lenses
- Drugs and pharmaceuticals
- Electric motors
- Pesticide formulators
- Photographic sensitised paper
- Razor blades
- Collapsible tubes etc.

As per MSME Annual Report 2013-14 there are 46 Million MICRO, Small and Medium Sector enterprises across various industries employing 106 Million people.

Table 5.1

Classification of SMEs according to Micro, Small and Medium Enterprises Development Act, 2006

Type of enterprise	Engaged in manufacture or production of goods Investment in plant and machinery	Engaged in providing or rendering of services Investment in equipment
Micro enterprise	Does not exceed 25 lakh rupees	Does not exceed 10 lakh rupees
Small enterprise	More than 25 lakh rupees, but does not exceed 5 crore rupees	More than 10 lakh rupees but does not exceed 2 crore rupees
Medium enterprise	More than 5 crore rupees but does not exceed 10 crore rupees	More than 2 crore rupees but does not exceed 5 crore rupees

5.1.3 Characteristics of SMEs

The characteristics of SMEs in the process of establishment and development are mostly reflected in the following aspects.

1. **First**, it's simple to create and the organic composition of capital is comparatively small. On the whole, SMEs have a relative shortage of venture capital and working capital. Thus, the scale of production of a capital is somewhat minor. Simultaneously, because of the lack of funds and employees, SMEs usually cannot simply get involved in the industry which comparatively has a high cost of entry or exit.

2. **Second**, it is hard to finance and be self-sufficient. In comparison with other big companies, SMEs are more difficult in financing in the start-up phase due to its lack of favourable financial information and its low credit level. In this phase, the industrialists are usually financing themselves, such as their own personal savings or taking a loan from friends. If the investment ventures of small and medium enterprises belong to the field of high-tech, venture capitalists will think about investing; venture capitalists will invest a small amount of money, but they will need high returns.

3. **Third**, the possession and operation rights are not divided. Even if SMEs (small and medium enterprises) acquire venture capital, it is restricted to SMEs in high-tech industry, and only some enterprises can get the support. Thus, SMEs are mainly funded by self-financing, so that both the ownership and the rights of management are determined. For the majority of small enterprises, the entrepreneurs are also the proprietors of the enterprise's assets.

4. **Fourth**, the management has a simple structure. SMEs operators take pleasure in business decision-making so, there is no need to make a complex organisational structure. In the early phase of SMEs, financial difficulties also compelled the enterprise to keep the management structure simple so as to decrease the costs. The simplicity of management organisation can be seen in the organisational structure, concentrated decision-making authority and the merger of ownership and management.

5. **Fifth**, the enterprise is frequently with strong well-known features. For the most part, SMEs establishment and governance are built because of some kind of similarity. Although this relationship is not a formal contract, it plays a significant role in the internal governance process. But this relationship will lead to some bad results, for example, cronyism; some of the employees broke the rules by virtue of their "royalty" status, decision-making power; command rights and supervision rights are not clearly demarcated by the lack of internal control.

6. **Sixth**, growth has important phases. Although enterprises have a lifecycle, the phases are not completely different in general business. But for SMEs, their growth frequently has monthly features. Generally, SMEs that are successful go through four phases: the Seed Stage, the Start-up Stage, the Expansion Stage and the Mature Stage. SMEs at different development phases have different features such as the source of value, capital structure, return on investment, business model, risk connotation, level of risk, cash flow. Incidentally, this situation gives rise to venture capitalists' phased investment, so that the risk investment has flexible characteristics so as to avoid more losses. However, this circumstance determines that management control for SMEs should choose a correct way in accordance with the stage characteristics.

7. **Seventh**, there are features such as weak competitiveness, difficult operations and high elimination rates. It is affected a great deal by the market and external shocks. Because of the small production scale of the SMEs, production technology is generally worse than that of big enterprises, which causes a huge wastage in resources.

The enterprise has low value-added products and technologies, and most of them belong to the imitation industry. The value that is inbuilt in the product is mainly human labour, lacking brand effect. It is not easy for small companies to struggle with big enterprises and foreign-funded enterprises with higher technology and a perfect sales network.

5.1.4 Contents of Management Control in Small and Medium Enterprises

The important factor limiting the development of SMEs is funds and intellectual capitals including human capital. So, the management control of SMEs should concentrate on financial and human resources. The content of management control in SMEs mostly consists of the following three aspects.

1. Marketing Control

The first in marketing control. Marketing control is the tool for ensuring that the marketing programme and activities of the form always get directed toward the marketing objectives of the firm, four important element emerge which constitute the marketing control process. These are: formulation of performance standard, performance appraisal, correction of derivation and plan reformulation. Tools and techniques of marketing control are marketing conduit. Marketing cost analysis, Credit Control, Market Share Analysis, Budgetary Control, Contribution Marketing Analysis, Management by Objectives (MBO) etc.

2. Financial Control

The second is financial control. It is important to manage and examine the obtainment, delivery, expenses, revenue and distribution of the funds frequently, and correct deviations.

In accordance with the SMEs' own features and the issues of external environment, the financing channels for SMEs are comparatively limited. It is not easy to raise funds by issuing shares or bonds, taking a loan from banks and so on. The absence of funds has turned out to be the blockage of SMEs' growth. So it becomes a difficult problem to acquire the funds and to use the funds effectively. This problem is accompanied with the growing process of SMEs and they are required to solve it. Therefore, for SMEs, the financial control should mainly consist of, to control the financing and investment, the usage of fixed capital and liquidity, the earnings and the rational allocation of funds. The goal of financial control is to speed up the turnover of cash flow gold and attain capital value-adding.

3. Human Resources Control

The third is the control of human resources. In SMEs, particularly in high-tech SMEs, instead of financial capital, intellectual capital is the major source of value and driving the main factor of value is human capital, structural capital and social network capital. Human capital refers to the knowledge, experience and operational capacity to solve customer issues. Amongst three kinds of intellectual capital, human capital is the important factor. On the one hand, because the information is concealed from the people, the delivery of information should be completed by human behaviour. Thus, the enterprise should establish an incentive mechanism to reflect the potential of human resources and make implicit information explicit and become the resource of value. However, as the intellectual capital has the characteristic of running off, together with the leave of the employees, managers play significant roles in the process of change that form intellectual capitals to the permanent capital. So, in order to create importance, SMEs should control intellectual capitals and human resources' control is the main element of intellectual capital control.

5.1.5 Methodology of Implementing Management Control Systems

Management control process is mostly behavioural. It involves communication among managers and their subordinates. Managers vary in their technical abilities, their leadership styles, their interpersonal skills, their experiences, their approach in decision-making, their attitudes towards the entity, their likes or dislikes for numbers and different other ways. Due to these differences, the details of management control process differ among firms and among the responsible centres in a firm.

However, the formal management control system is essentially the same all through the organisation; the differences mainly relate to how the system is used. For example, managers vary in their attitude towards the relative importance. A specific amount of each is important.

The sequence in which the control process takes place has been identified as follows.

1. Strategic planning
2. Budget preparation.
3. Management control of operations
4. Analysing performance reports and evaluating managerial performance
5. Management compensation as it relates to management control process

1. Strategic Planning

Most of the firm's managers spend a lot of time thinking about the future, which leads to an informal understanding of the future direction in which the entity is going, or it might be a formal statement of specific plans about how to go there. Such a formal statement of plans is called strategic planning. Strategic planning is the process of determining the programmes that the organisation will carry out and on the estimated amount of resources that will be assigned to each program over the next number of years.

2. Budget Preparation

Budgets are a significant tool for successful short-term planning and control in a company. An operating budget generally covers one year and states the revenues and costs planned for that year. It has the following features –

(a) A budget estimates the profit potential of a business unit.

(b) It is stated in monetary terms although the monetary amounts may be supported by non-monetary amounts (for example, units sold or produced).

(c) It usually covers the period of one year but quarterly breakups, especially those that are affected by seasonal factors.

(d) It is a management commitment; managers agree to accept responsibility for achieving the budgeted goals.

(e) The budget proposal is re-examined and approved by an authority higher than the budgeter and finally, by the Chief Executive Officer (CEO).

(f) Once approved, the budget can be changed under special conditions.

(g) At regular intervals, the actual financial performance is compared to the budget and differences are analysed and explained.

The process of preparing budget should be differentiated from (a) strategic planning and (b) forecasting.

3. Management Control of Operations

Management control is working through others, so that the work can be completed effectively. Managers do not control costs; what managers do is to control the actions of individuals, who are accountable for incurring the costs. The manager chooses the employees and ensures that they are sufficiently trained, decides where they fit best in the organisation, gives advice, suggestions, resolves arguments within the liable centres, approves suggested actions that the employees are authorised to use their own authorities, communicates with other managers to get their support and to resolve problems when their activities hinder the work of the responsible centre and especially, seeks to create a part that persuades the employees to work effectively. To continue with these activities, managers require information which is recognised as:

Formal Information

(i) **Task control information:** A production control system gives information that plans the flow of material, labour and other resources, so the correct finished goods in the correct quantities appear at the end of the production.

(ii) **Budget reports:** The budget that is accepted is the recommended financial device for controlling the activities of the responsibility centre and a report that compares the original revenues and costs with budgeted amounts is the main element of the report.

(iii) **Non-financial information:** Sales rise in units as well as in rupees. Others are reported because the information may need a quick action. These are called as key variables bookings, back orders market share, key actual numbers, capacity utilisation, quality, on time delivery, inventory turnover. Recent developments that have influenced the management control system, consist of just-in-time systems, total quality control, computer integrated manufacturing and decision support systems.

4. Analysing performance reports and evaluating managerial performance

Performance measures are a central part of management information and reporting system. It handles performance measures for different levels of an organisation and for managers at these levels.

Performance measurements of organisation units should be a requirement for assigning resources within that organisation. When a unit carries out new tasks of revenues, costs and investments are prepared. An ongoing comparison of the original revenues, costs and investments with the budgeted amounts can assist in directing top management's decisions about future allotments.

Performance measurement of a manager is used in decisions about their salaries, bonus, future assignments and status, which encourage the managers to try hard for the goals used in their assessment.

Table 5.2: Five Level Performance Measures

Representative Area at which Data is Gathered	Financial Measures	Non-Financial Measures
1. Customer / Market level	(i) Prices of company's products compared with competition. (ii) Prices of company's traded securities.	(i) Market share held by company's products. (ii) Third party quality. ratings for all products in the industry.
2. Total organisational level	(i) Return on investment (ROI) (ii) Residual income (RI)/EVA (iii) Return on sales cost and revenue measurements for each responsibility centre according to measure of performance used (that is cost, revenue, profit, and return on investments). This is known as responsibility accounting. Financial measures include flexible budget variances.	(i) Number of new products introduced. (ii) Number of new patents filed.

contd. ...

3. Individual facility level (includes manufacturing plants, distribution, sales, customer service centres, and R&D centre).		(i) Capacity utilisation. (ii) Throughput time for products. (iii) Percentage of times promised delivery dates met (schedule attainment).
4. Individual activity level (for example, activities in a warehouse facility include receiving, storing, dispatching etc.)	(i) Direct material variance and direct labour variances. (ii) Manufacturing overhead variances. (iii) Cost per activity level.	(i) Time taken to set up machinery for new production run. (ii) No. of accounts receivables processed per hour. (iii) Inventory level not to exceed certain amounts. (iv) Abiding by plant maintenance schedules. Time period for completion, that is, break even time is the time from initial idea date to the time when the cumulative present value of cash inflows of the project equals the present value of total (to market) cash outflows.
5. By Product / Programme	Cost and revenues and investments across responsibility centres as far as they pertain to program or product (compares to budgeted / target amounts). This is sometimes referred to as activity costing.	

Performance Reports: Format and Essential Features

(a) **Tailored to the organisation structure and controllability:** The performance report system should be planned according to the organisation structure of the enterprise, the same way as budgeting and accounting systems. There should be a separate performance report for each responsibility centre, beginning with those at the lowest level which consecutively provide summary reports for each higher level.

(b) **Designed to implement the exception principle in management:** Performance report must plainly differentiate between controllable and non-controllable items. Performance measurement needs the original results to compare it with the plans, goals and standards so that differences attract the management's attention to high, low and satisfactory performance. The differences from plans indicate the need for enquiry and possible action. The action may be corrective, commendatory or provisory. Both favourable and unfavourable differences justify the enquiry. Unfavourable differences may indicate danger further enquiry is required to pinpoint the exact cause.

(c) **Repetitive:** Performance should be repetitive, normally on a monthly basis, although certain problems may imply the need for weekly or even daily reports that concentrate on a specific problem.

(d) **Adapted to the requirements of the principal user:** Performance reports serve the assessment and decision-making requirements of the user.

   (i) Top management must have reports that give a full and comprehensive summary of the general features of operations and an identification of major events. The summaries should be supported by sufficient detail to facilitate tracing bad situations to their source.

   (ii) Middle management is generally defined as those members of management responsible for major sub-divisions of the company such as sales, production and finance. Middle management is responsible for performing the responsibilities allotted to the sub-divisions within the broad policies and goals established by top management. Performance reports for middle management, although including summary data, are also characterised by comprehensive information on daily operations.

   (iii) Lower level management (supervisors and foreman) is mainly concerned with synchronisation and control of daily operations; therefore controlled reports should be designed consequently. Reports to foreman and supervisors must be easy to understand and limited to items having a direct bearing on the supervisor's operational responsibilities.

    (i) Written: (a) Formal financial statement

                      (b) Tabulated statistics

                      (c) Narration and exposition using words

    (ii) Graphic: (a) Charts

                      (b) Diagrams and pictures

    (iii) Oral: (a) Group meetings

                      (b) Conferences with individuals

(iv) Many top executives have a strong preference for narrative summaries of internal reports. Words often tell the story much more efficiently than base figures. Analysis of the causative factors involved, for instance, in a performance report indicating important exceptions, usually should be presented in a descriptive form.

(v) Oral presentation should be an important element of the internal reporting system in all firms. The controller and budget directors should motivate the use of executive conferences where the performance report is presented, explained and talked about. Oral presentation is significant because interpretation and emphasis is possible that are absent in other types.

(e) Simple, understandable and report only essential information: Reports should not be very long; tabulations that are difficult should be avoided. Reports should be carefully monitored to remove all unnecessary information. Several performance reports contain a lot of information rather than too little.

Performance reports must be regulated. An executive becomes used to specific terminology, forms and techniques of presentation and knows where to look to find the particular data. In spite of the attraction of standardising performance reports, continuous attention should be given to improving them. Improvement essentially involved changes, but desirable changes, if made at a favourable time and effectively presented, can be achieved generally with a least amount of confusion. Reports must be kept relevant.

(f) Prepared and presented promptly: In agreement with the cost of a comprehensive record keeping and reporting, performance reports should be available on time. To attain a realistic balance between immediate reporting and the costs of detailed reporting, monthly performance reports are extensively used by industry. When special problem areas are involved, weekly and even on a daily basis, reporting may be required, at least for a time.

(g) Effective management follow-up procedures: Follow-up procedures form an important aspect of effective control. Some firms need written explanations of important variances. The follow-up processes that are preferred by other firms involve constructive meetings where the causes are examined and corrective action is determined upon.

(i) Follow-up processes must start at the top management level in the executive committee meeting, for example, where both poor and adequate conditions are talked about and analysed. Decisions should be made regarding ways and means of correcting poor conditions.

(ii) Variances that are preferable should be granted equivalent study, (1) to decide whether the goals were realistic and (2) to give credit to those accountable for high performances, and (3) possibly to transfer some "know-how" to other subdivisions of the firm.

(iii) Group and individual conference should be conducted at different management levels for effective correction action. Follow-up processes should represent constructive action to change the adverse conditions rather than punitive action for failures, the results of which obviously cannot be erased.

(iv) Another significant aspect of follow-up process is that the resulting action is just a line of responsibility rather than a staff responsibility. The budget director, controller or other staff officer should not carry out nor be given, the responsibility of imposing the budget.

(v) To have the maximum advantage, the monthly report should be planned to show the performance of each person having supervisory responsibility. A good designed control report should be fully incorporated, that is, each schedule should look on a responsibility basis so that (i) major deviation may be mapped to the source of the problem, and (ii) the different sections include within themselves a full report.

(vi) Distribution of the monthly performance report should basically follow the similar pattern as the annual profit budget plan. Certain executives require the full monthly performance report. Other members of the management only require those schedules that are connected to their particular responsibility centres. Lower levels of management may get only one of the comprehensive sections. However, the higher the level of management, the greater the need for summaries, yet these summaries should be supported by sufficient detail to recognise specific aspects of operations.

5. Management Compensation

Every organisation has different objectives. A significant role of management control systems is to encourage organisational members to achieve those objectives. This chapter concentrates on incentive mechanisms and compensation systems and their purpose in controlling the behaviour of employees, as they search for goal compatibility. Managers normally put a lot of effort on activities that are rewarded and a smaller amount on activities that are not rewarded. There are several examples of compensation systems that do not reward behaviour that help in achieving the organisational goals or that reward behaviour contradicting these goals.

The key to encouraging people to behave in a way that develops an organisation's goals lies in the way the organisation's incentives connect to the individuals' goals. People are influenced by both positive and negative incentives. A positive incentive, or "reward", is a result that increases satisfaction of individual requirements. On the other hand, a negative incentive, or "punishment," is a result that reduces satisfaction of those requirements. Reward incentives are inducements to satisfy the requirements that people cannot acquire without joining the organisation. Organisations reward participants who perform in the ways that has been decided. Research on incentives tends to support the following.

(a) People tend to be more strongly encouraged by the potential of earning rewards than by fearing punishment, which proposes that management control systems should be reward-oriented.

(b) A personal reward is relative or situational. Monetary compensation is a significant means of fulfilling different requirements beyond a particular satisfaction level, on the other hand, the amount of compensation is not essentially as significant as non-monetary rewards.

(c) If senior management indicates by its actions that it considers the management control system as significant, operating managers will also consider it as significant. If senior management does not focus much on the system, operating managers will follow suit.

(d) People are highly inspired when they get reports, or feedback, about their performance. Without such feedback, individuals are not likely to feel a sense of accomplishment or self-realisation or to understand how they can alter their behaviour to meet their goals.

(e) Incentives become less effective as the time between an action and feedback on it rises. At lower levels in the organisation, the optimal frequency may be just hours; for senior management, it may be months.

(f) Motivation is weakest when the person considers an incentive is either unachievable or too easily achievable. Motivation is strong when it takes some effort to achieve the goal and when the person considers this achievement as significant in relation to his or her requirements.

(g) The incentive that a budget or other statement of objective provides is strongest when managers work with their superiors to attain the budgeted amounts.

Objectives, goals, or standards will probably provide strong incentive only if the manager perceives them as just and is committed in achieving them. The commitment is strongest when it is a matter of public record, that is, when the manager has clearly decided that the budgeted amounts are achievable.

5.1.6 Tools and Techniques for Implementing Management Control Systems

Almost all management control systems show a planning and review cycle. The time perspective for this is significant, as different control situations can justify everything from cycles running for many years to day-to-day re-thinking and planning. **Nilsson** and **Olive** (2001) used words such as "preferences", "knowledge" and "dialogues" to remind us of the strategic discussion regarding what is attractive and possible. The diagram should be deduced as shopping that the discussion is ongoing and frequently turning out targets and plans, which are then visualised to form the basis for action. "Communicating and linking" explains the significance of forming a cohesive picture of what the tasks are and how they fit together.

The planning and review procedures use many different tools. Some tools are basically models, while others are techniques. In the introductory definition of management control, "formalised information-based routines, structures and processes" was discussed. A significant part of the design of these is choosing and adapting the control tools that are to be used. We have selected to talk about this from a general viewpoint on the basis of the metrics used to visualise the strategy, and how these will then, in the form of information and incentives, form decisions and responsibilities.

(A) Reward Systems

Reward systems are a main motivational tool to protect the participation of people to attain organisational goals. It is a common belief that only the employees of an organisation are entitled to rewards. Organisations on the other hand, also reward their stakeholders – customers, stockholders, creditors, and the public for their contribution. Reward systems are a significant source of communication and feedback. They express what the company expects of a person. Rewards create a sense of belonging which makes a person feel more committed towards his work. Reward systems go with the interests of stakeholders and managers.

A manager's total compensation package is made up of three components:

- Salary
- Benefits
- Incentives

(B) Transfer Pricing

Another significant feature of management control systems is transfer pricing. It is one of the most significant issues in the strategic and operational management practices of big business companies. There is perhaps no single accounting subject that uses more management time and energy than the business of setting up acceptable transfer prices. Transfer pricing is used by decentralised transnational companies as a strategic tool to deal with the issues of brand creation.

The strategic objectives of international transfer pricing fall into three areas – taxation-related objectives, internal management-oriented objectives, and international or operational objectives. The pricing of internal transactions carried out by multi-national enterprise (MNE) headquarters is a tax issue that tax authorities are worried about, but it is also a strategic concern of MNEs in supporting its local subsidiaries on brand creation and output decision, as the MNEs have the incentive to control their transfer prices so as to move profit cross-border. In addition to a tax-driven mechanism, transfer pricing is frequently used by the enterprise in attaining competitive advantage and other strategic objectives as well.

Transfer price is the internal value placed on a raw material, good, or service as it moves from one connected organisational unit to another within a united corporate group. Transfer price models help in rational distribution of shared costs when the products and services are exchanged between independent sections within a decentralised organisation. Transfer pricing mechanism can also be misused by moving profits in case of organisations working under inconsistent tax jurisdictions. Some even think that transfer price is more of a strategy rather than a process.

(C) Budgeting as a Control Mechanism

One of the conventional management control systems is the budgeting process, which has served as the main internal measurement of performance. Conventional budgetary control is proving more and more inappropriate for the rapidly changing environment of the modern business world. During the course of a budget year, budgets are quickly becoming out-dated. Several organisations state the budget is already outdated at the beginning of the budget period because of the time taken to put it together. Even if there have been attempts to keep budgets new by more frequent revisions the general experience is that it is hard to concentrate on annual financial targets during the revision procedures. Budgeting is proving to be a very limited management tool, and at times is made more inflexible by linking performance bonuses to budget achievement.

Traditional budgeting has served as means of highlighting boundary systems that concentrate on financial limits and diagnostic controls. Budgets show the limits of spending on particular categories and variance reporting serves to show conformity with these standards. As such, budgeting serves as a tool of corporate governance.

Top management sets forth spending instructions. Individual/group assessments are based on cost control and adherence with standards. In order for employees to be better associated with the organisation's strategic goals, budgets are used to highlight the organisation's core beliefs and important interactive controls. The focus of budget has moved away from simple governance mechanism towards creating value. Corporate value creation is reliant on the organisation's capability to develop and grow important resources. The management must pass on core strategic values and develop an incorporated set of financial and non-financial measures to assess progress. The role of finance has changed over the past ten years. Financial managers are trying to go away from score keeping and variance analysis towards risk analysis and integration, thus changing the nature of budgeting.

In present times, many multinational companies have included non-financial factors into the planning process and are replacing annual budgeting and instead are accepting rolling budgets. The budgetary slack remains as one of the major concerns in practise, referring to the practice of deliberate underestimation of revenues and overestimation of costs. The goal transparency decreases managerial dysfunctional behaviour in budgeting activities. His research on the other hand did not find any important association with goal difficulties and tendency to create budgetary slack.

The manager's value orientation towards innovation has an impact and can influence organisational commitment. The effect of increasing decentralisation plus budgetary participation on organisational commitment is considerably stronger for managers with high value orientation towards innovation. It is thus significant for an organisation to consider the features of the manager's value orientations, the organisations structure and its core control system when considering designing a control system in an organisation.

(D) Balanced Scorecard

One the most significant ways to control and measure the performance of an organisation is a Balanced Scorecard (BSC) that was first introduced by Kaplan and Norton in 1992, as a model for executing strategy. The main thrust of the BSC is that it is usually unsuitable to try to supervise using financial measures of performance alone. Financial measures are required to be added by other non-financial performance measures and also by various important indicators of future performance, which are generally non-financial in nature.

The BSC is designed to be a strategic management tool that allows organisations to interpret strategic goals into related measures of performance. Financial and non-financial measures are indicators of the extent that strategies are effectively being executed throughout the organisation and whether strategic goals are being attained.

The BSC measures performance from four perspectives, namely the financial perspective, the customer perspective, the internal business process perspective and the learning and growth perspective. The BSC interprets the organisation's performance measures that intersect conventional functional areas. The progress towards attaining short-term and long-term goals is measured by outcome-based and leading indicator and driver-oriented indicators. BSC implementation represents a way that organisations try to fulfil the demands of the capital markets.

The fundamental goals of the BSC are to express top management's strategic idea. An incorporated set of measures directs managers towards generating favourable results for executing strategy. This incorporation finally assists managers in developing a model for knowing the company within its surroundings.

In small medium enterprises many important management challenges, particularly in the execution stage of BSC were recognised. These may comprise processes owners not being ready, resistance to change, absence of training, lack of synchronisation between departments and shortage of funds. The strength of a structured mechanical approach is of greatest significance to SMEs with limited resources.

(E) Benchmarking and Bench Trending

Benchmarking is a constant process of comparing products and operations with the strongest competitors or the best practices in related operations of the best performing firm. Benchmarking is a process that is contrary to the conventional technique of establishing existing goals on the basis of past performance of the organisation. Target costing is a certain form of benchmarking applied to product costs.

The benchmarking consists of four sub-processes:

1. **Planning the variables to be benchmarked and selecting the companies that are to be used for comparison and methods used to collect comparative data on these companies:** The first thing is to determine the benchmarking variables such as products manufactured, services given, products or services bought, processes used, major costs variables etc. The next step is to recognise the targeted firms such as competitors, identical functions in the similar firm or same functions in firms out of the industry. Companies with the best practices can be recognised through internal and external sources, including built-up data bases, professional alliances, industry studies, journals, trade publications, consultants, contacts, seminars, vendors and company sponsored surveys.

The generic benchmarking process is shown in Fig. 5. 1.

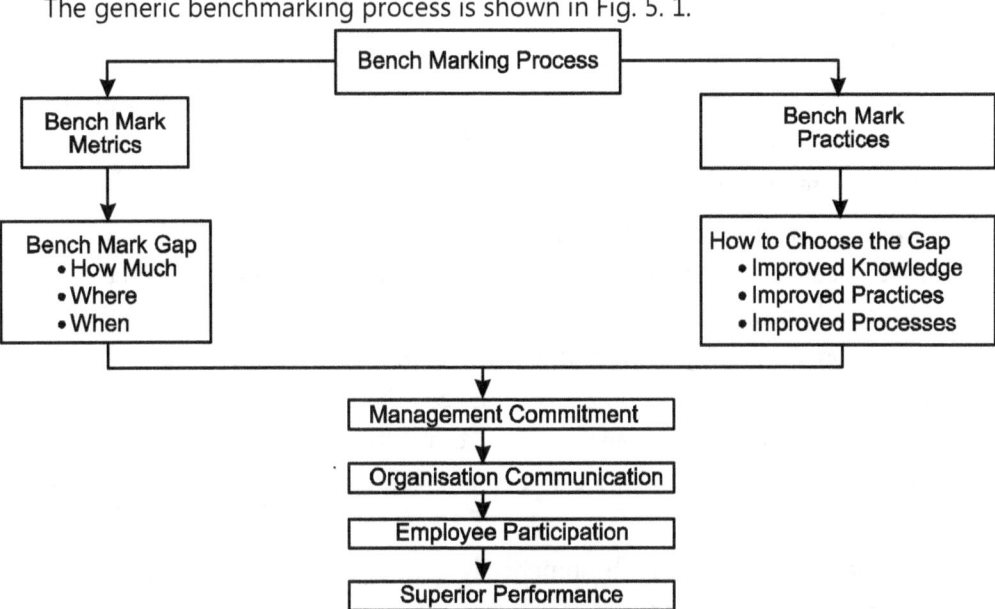

Fig. 5.1: Generic Benchmarking Process

2. **Establish the current and projected gap in performance between the target company's operations and internal operations:** The reason for the analysis stage is to decide the existing gap in performance between present internal operations and best practices and to show the possible future gap if nothing is completed. Best practices can be established on the basis of clear superiority, expert judgement or repeated occurrences of best practices in many circumstances. It is significant to show the possible future gap, since practices change eventually.

   The benchmarking studies generally give useful information about the gaps in competitiveness for a function or process. Bench trading studies include a projection of the important market and customer structural variables such as identification of customer preferences, innovation threats, new entrants, geopolitical impacts and other market variables that are important for the long-term success for the company. The methods connected to bench trending is same as benchmarking but with new structural measurements. Management should determine when the extra effort needed to perform bench trending is beneficial.

3. **Communicating benchmark findings to operating personnel and establishing internal goals for implementation:** The gap may be closed by two kinds of actions – strategic actions and continuous operating actions. Certain goals with correct time frame must be set for closing it and appropriate communication to all concerned, that is, marketing, new business development, business management, engineering, manufacturing management, and controller.

(F) Just-in-Time Technique

'Just-in-time' as the name shows, signifies that at the extreme there is zero inventory and products are produced or ordered only when they are required. Even if the extreme case is unusual, the word is a popular way of defining the direction.

The following are just-in-time techniques used –

(i) **Reducing buffer inventory at each workstation:** Buffer inventory exists to a certain extent because workstations stop working and sometimes because they produce substandard products. When these events happen production in the following workstation stops unless there is inventory that they can draw. Steps to decrease machine breakdown and improve quality will decrease the keeping of buffer inventory. Buffer inventory also results from bottlenecks, that is, sluggish work in a number of workstations. This can be removed by balancing the output of many workstations.

(ii) **Decrease set-up costs:** With numerically controlled machine tools, set-up involves only adding a new computer programme in a machine. Thus, after the computer programme has been formed, the cost of setting up for the next and all following lots is small.

(iii) **Decrease procurement costs**: Rather than going through the long process of requesting bids from vendors, analysing bids, placing order with the best vendor, and receiving and checking the incoming goods, some firms have established relations with one or two vendors for each item and they want the vendor to deliver quality goods at a certain date.

(iv) **Relations with customers:** The other side of the coin is to establish connection with the customers for automatic ordering.

The following are the implications for management control:

(i) WIP inventory becomes so unimportant that it can be ignored. The only inventories are for raw materials and finished goods and issue from raw materials inventory are charged directly to finished goods inventory. In fact, a job-cost system is changed into process-cost system. With only one cost centre and the boring task of calculating "equivalent production" (which is required to find WIP amounts when the inventory in a cost centre includes partly finished products) is removed, resulting in substantial decrease in record-keeping. Products are carried in inventory as standard costs without tracing actual costs to individual products.

(ii) It focuses the management attention on time as well as cost. One of the effective ways to check progress is to calculate the following ratio by establishing targets.

The best results can be acquired by stressing on continuous improvement in this ratio towards the ideal number of I, since only processing time adds value to the product.

$$\frac{\text{Processing time}}{\text{cycle time}} = \frac{\text{Processing time}}{\text{Processing time} + \text{Storage time} + \text{Movement time} + \text{Inspection time}}$$

(G) Computer Integrated Manufacturing

In petroleum refineries, chemical processing and similar processing plants, materials and energy enter in the beginning and at different stages of the process and the finished products appear at the end without involving any manpower. Human beings maintain the tools, check the quality of the process, and if it gets uncontrollable, close it down and bring it back into control. In the same way, product control systems in other industries also have experienced a change they have now come within reach of those found in process manufacturing. These developments include numerically controlled machine tools, robots and computers that assimilate the work of other computers. This has caused a decrease in manpower involvement, decrease in paper work, removal of duplicate record-keeping, inconsistencies of information in separate systems, decrease in inventory, and decrease in through-put time and resulting decrease in production costs.

Complex, costly computer systems are now used to link together different stages of production such as Manufacturing Resource Planning II (MRPII); Flexible Manufacturing System (FMS); Manufacturing Accounting and Production Information Control Systems (mapics) ii), Manufacturing Resource Planning and Execution System (MRPX) and Computer Aided Manufacturing (CAM). These systems integrate into a single system all or at least many of the previous separate systems for product design, order processing, accounts receivable, payroll, accounts payable, inventory control, bills of materials, capacity planning, product scheduling and product cost accounting.

The following are the implications of management control process –

(i) **Increase in task control:** The system that is completely developed changes particular production activities that once needed management control.

(ii) **Better information:** The systems give information more precisely more constantly, with more detail and at much less cost than the systems they supersede.

(iii) **More prompt information:** Information is available shortly after the event occurs and in some cases almost instantly.

(iv) **Work teams:** Under the newer systems, performance focuses on the performance of the whole team.

(v) **Business unit controller:** One result of the team approach is that business unit controller should be made mainly accountable for helping the business unit manager in planning and controlling the units' operations.

(H) Target Costing

Target cost is the maximum manufacturing cost of a product. Target costing is done to motivate different design and production departments to find less costly ways of attaining similar or better product characteristics and quality. It is decided after analysing market niches, evaluating customer needs, understanding cost drivers, determining elasticity of demand, and analysing volume-cost relationships. It is estimated by deducting the expected market price from the required margin on sales.

Target costing goes through three stages. They are:

- Planning stage
- Development stage
- Production stage

(L) Activity-Based Costing (ABC)

In the last few years, there have been numerous changes in the collection and utilisation of cost information due to increased computerisation and automation in factories. Conventionally, costs were allotted to products, on the basis of the direct labour hours. But today, firms presently are stressing on dividing material-related costs from other manufacturing costs. The manufacturing costs are collected separately for individual departments and machines which carry out a series of operations that are ultimately included to get the final product. Here, the direct labour cost is added to the other costs which results in conversion costs. Conversion costs are comprised of the factory and labour overhead costs of changing raw materials into finished goods. The newer cost systems also contain the administrative costs, R&D costs and marketing costs. These systems use numerous allotment bases. Here the word 'activity' is used to show "cost centre" and "cost driver," and not on the basis of resource distribution. Thus, this cost system is called as activity-based cost system.

As a strategic planning tool, ABC assists in knowing the effectiveness of products. It has numerous strategic and tactical uses in an organisation. It helps to

- Recognise the values of the organisation's activities, business segments, etc. through a comprehensive knowledge of costs and related dynamics to help organisations focus attention on target outcomes;
- Recognise opportunities to successfully use delivery channels to improve outputs;
- Distinguish between activities given to different customer sections;
- Recognise incremental operating expenses so as to support growth;
- Recognise cost management opportunities;
- Give information to improve process efficiency.

5.1.7 Roles and Responsibilities in Implementing Management Control

Different management control activities that allow an individual to perform many activities are given in detail below:

1. Planning what the organisation should do.
2. Synchronising the activities of the many parts of the organisation.
3. Communicating information.
4. Evaluating information.
5. Deciding what, if any, action should be taken.
6. Influencing people to change the behaviour.

Management control does not essentially mean that actions should correspond to a plan, such as budget. The stated plans based on situations prevailing both inside and outside the organisation, were believed to exist. If the situations are now thought to be different, the planned action may no longer be suitable. Management control by contrast, should expect what circumstances are going to be in future.

The reason of management control is to make sure that strategies are performed so that the organisation's goals are accomplished. If a manager finds out a better way of working rather than what actions are mentioned in the plan, to attain organisation's goals then the management control system should not forbid him from working in that style. In particular cases the manager is required to get consent for such departure.

Goal Congruence

The function of every organisation is to achieve its goals. The goals are achieved by the CEO, with the recommendation of other members of senior management and generally ratified by the Board of Directors. In several eminent organisations, the goals initially set by the founder continue for generations.

In a formal management control system in an organisation, profitability generally is the most significant goal. Profitability refers to profits in the long run. Some CEOs concentrate on revenue because they think size itself is a goal. Maximising shareholder value may be another goal. Other non-financial goals may be organisation effectiveness, high productivity, good organisational leadership, high morale, good organisational reputation, high organisational efficiency, organisational growth, organisational stability, and value to local community and service to the public. Financial goals clearly portray a specified return on investment and specified earnings per share.

The central reason for a management control system is to guarantee, as much as possible, direct people to take actions in line with their self-interest as also in the best interest of the organisation. This is the principle of goal congruence.

Tools for Implementing Strategy

Management control systems help managers move an organisation towards its strategic goals. Thus, management control concentrates mainly on strategy implementation.

Management control is only one of the tools managers use in implementing desired strategies. Strategies can be implemented all the way through the organisation structure, its management of human relations and its particular culture. These are shown in Fig. 5.2.

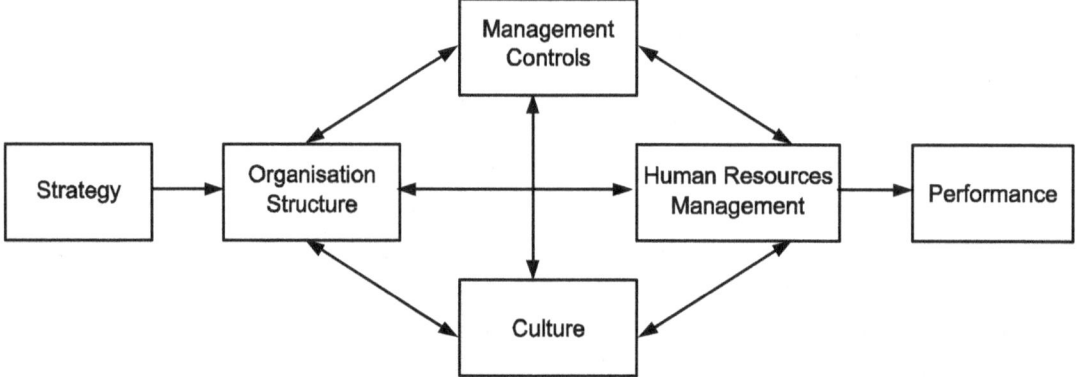

Fig. 5.2: Framework for Strategy Implementation

The complete framework for strategy implementation is explained as follows –

1. **Organisation Structure:** Organisation structure establishes the roles, reporting relationships and divisions of responsibilities that form decision-making in an organisation.

2. **Human Resource Management:** Human resources management is the selection, training, evaluation, promotion and termination of employees so as to increase the knowledge and skills needed to implement organisational strategy.

3. **Culture:** Culture refers to the set of common beliefs, attitudes and norms that explicitly or implicitly guide managerial actions.

4. **Financial and Non-financial Emphasis:** Management control system includes both financial and non-financial performance measures. The financial dimension concentrates on the monetary "bottom line" net income after tax, return on equity and so forth. But there are non-financial goals as well such as product quality, market share, customer satisfaction, on-time delivery and employee morale.

5. **Aid in Developing New Strategies:** As discussed earlier, the main role of management control is to guarantee implementation of selected strategies. In industries where environment is changing quickly, management control information especially of non-financial nature can provide a basis for considering new strategies. This is called as interactive control. Interactive control calls management attention to developments both negative and positive that show the need for new strategic initiatives.

5.2 Management Control Structure

5.2.1 Introduction

Management control system is an organised methodical process and structure to facilitate optimum utilisation of resources that a manager does effectively in achieving organisational goals. The organisational objective stipulates a realistic and well-defined goal to lay foundation for strategic planning organisational structure and control processes. The dimensions of management control are related to and influenced by organisational structures which have a structural progression on strategy-structure-process relationship on business renderings.

Organisation structure is the formal definition of the lines of responsibility and authority and communication channels among different levels of hierarchy in management. The structure of the organisation divides the task among people for efficiency and clarity, and synchronise between the independent parts of the organisation to guarantee organisational effectiveness. Structure balances the need for specialisation with the need for integration. The choice of structure must be decided by the company's strategy. This structure must segment key activities and/or strategic operating units to improve efficiency through specialisation, response to a competitive environment and freedom to act. Simultaneously, the structure must effectively put together and synchronise these activities and units to accommodate interdependence of activities for complete control. The choice of structure reflects strategy in terms of the company's

(i)   Size

(ii) Product/service diversity

(iii) Competitive environment and volatility, and

(iv) Internal political consideration and information/co-ordination needs for each component

Simultaneously, the principal criterion for all decisions on organisation structure and behaviour should be their importance to the attainment of the organisational purpose, not their agreement to the orders of special disciplines.

The management control system is the whole organisation system and is more positive-oriented. The structure of management control system is generally built around a financial structure, where organisation resources and activities are conveyed regarding monetary units. The mixed resources are activities of organisation which can be used in combinations to make an organisational unit and the job is fixed to achieve one or more purposes, which is generally known as 'responsibility centre'.

5.2.2 Responsibility Centre

The word responsibility centre is used to indicate any organisation unit that is headed by a responsible manager. Actually, a firm is a set of responsibility centres, represented by a box in the organisation chart. These responsibility centres form a hierarchy. At the lowest level in the organisation are responsibility centres for segments, work shifts or other small organisation units. At the highest level are departments or business units (divisions), and from a position of senior management and the board of directors, the entire firm is a responsibility centre, even if the word is generally used to refer to units within the firm.

A responsibility centre exists to achieve one or more purposes within the organisation goals and set strategies to attain these goals. The goals of the responsibility centres are to perform their part in executing these strategies.

A responsibility centre uses inputs, such as physical quantities of material, hours of different kinds of labour and variety of services. It requires working capital, equipment and other assets to do this work. Consequently, the responsibility centre produces outputs such as goods or services. The goods and services produced by a responsibility centre is given either to another responsibility centre as inputs or to the outside world, in which case they become outputs of the whole organisation and revenues are studied by selling these outputs.

Fig. 5.3 shows the essence of any responsibility centre.

Fig. 5.3: Responsibility Centre

5.2.3 Measurement of Performance of Responsibility Centre

There are the following distinct methods of measuring the performance of a responsibility centre –

1. **Relationship between inputs and outputs:** Management is accountable for guaranteeing the best relationship between inputs and outputs. In a number of centres the responsibility is informal and direct, as in the case of production department, for instance, inputs of raw materials become a part of the finished goods thus the control is concentrated on using a least amount of input required to produce the required output in accordance with the correct requirement and quality standards.

   In several circumstances, inputs are not directly connected to outputs. For example, advertising costs, though an input to increase sales revenue is just one of the several other factors. The relationship between increased advertising and any consequent increase in revenue is not always provable and the management's decision to raise advertising expenses is based on the judgement rather than the information. In the same way, the connection between inputs and outputs is even more unclear in case of R&D as the money spent on today's R&D may not be recognised for many years and thus the best sum any organisation should spent for R&D is indeterminable.

2. **Measuring inputs and outputs:** In a number of responsibility centres much of the input can be stated in physical terms – hours of labour, quarts of oil, reams of paper and kilowatt hours of electricity. In MCS (market communication system), these quantitative amounts are interpreted in financial terms. The financial value of a given input is normally calculated by increasing a physical quantity by a price per unit, for instance, hours of labour time's rate per hour, electricity cost by kilowatt hours x hourly rate the resulting monetary amount is known as cost and this is the way a responsibility centre input is usually conveyed.

   Inputs are the supplies that are used by the responsibility centre. Patients in a hospital or students in a school are not inputs. Rather, inputs are the supplies that the hospital or school uses to achieve the goal of treating the patients or educating the students.

   It is much simple to measure the cost of inputs than to calculate the value of outputs. Inputs such as R&D, human resources training, advertising and sales promotion may not have an effect on the output of the year in which cost is incurred. In such cases, outputs of such responsibility centres are not determined; the input cost is the measurement criteria.

3. **Efficiency:** Efficiency measure of performance pertains to setting standards regarding the amount of inputs used over a certain period of time for a specified level of output, and measure original performance against such standards. Examples are standards of labour and material that is established for a production function.

   The terms are occasionally used in a relative rather than in a complete sense. For example, responsibility centre A is more efficient than responsibility centre B either (a) if it uses fewer resource than responsibility centre B, but has a similar output or (b) if it uses the same amount of resources as responsibility centre B or has a greater output than responsibility centre B. In many responsibility centres, a measure of competence can be developed that relates the original costs to a similar standard, not a very precise measurement but only an estimate.

4. **Process as measurement of performance:** Here, the importance is the production process in the measure. Examples are the quality of production during a production process to deduce something about the quality of the final output before it is distributed or produced.

5. **Effectiveness as measure of performance:** Effectiveness is decided by the connection between the output of responsibility centre and its goals. The more this output contributes to the goals, the more successful the unit.

6. **The role of profit:** The key goals of any profit-oriented organisation are to make a good profit. Thus profit is a significant measure of effectiveness. Again since profits are the difference between revenue and expense it is also a measure of efficiency. Therefore, profit measures both effectiveness and efficiency.

5.2.4 Purpose of Responsibility Centre

The thought behind the hierarchy of responsibility centres and the responsibility accounting system is to distribute to the decentralised organisational entity, responsibility for different parts of ROI (return on investment). Each responsibility centre has allotted to it measures of performance that are suitable to the constituents of cost, quality, revenue and investment that are allocated to that responsibility centre. Rewards are made according to the performance. The combination of responsibility centres, measures of performance and rewards, joins together decentralised centres of decision-making in order to achieve overall organisational goal that comprise profit and ROI.

$$\text{ROI} = \frac{\text{Net Operating Profit}}{\text{Invested Capital}} = \frac{\text{Net Operating Profit}}{\text{Sales Revenue}} \times \frac{\text{Sales Revenue}}{\text{Invested Capital}}$$

= Net operating profit as a percentage of sales revenue x turnover of investment in relation to sales revenue

Net operating profit, that is, profit arising out of operations = Net profit before interest

One significant objective in a profit-oriented organisation is to make profits and the amount of profit, is a significant measure of efficiency. As profit is the difference between revenue and expense, profit also is a measure of efficiency. Therefore profit measures both effectiveness and efficiency.

5.2.5 Types of Responsibility Centres

There are at least four different types of responsibility centres classified in accordance with the nature of the monetary inputs and outputs that are measured for control purposes; revenue centres, expense centres, profit centres and investment centres. Their features are shown in Fig. 5.4.

1. In revenue centres, output is measured in monetary terms.

2. In expense centres, inputs are measured in monetary terms.

3. In profit centres, both revenues (output) and expenses (input) are measured.

4. In investment centres, the relationship between profit and investment is measured.

The planning and control systems for responsibility centres will be different depending on whether they are revenue centres, expense centres, profit centres and investment centres.

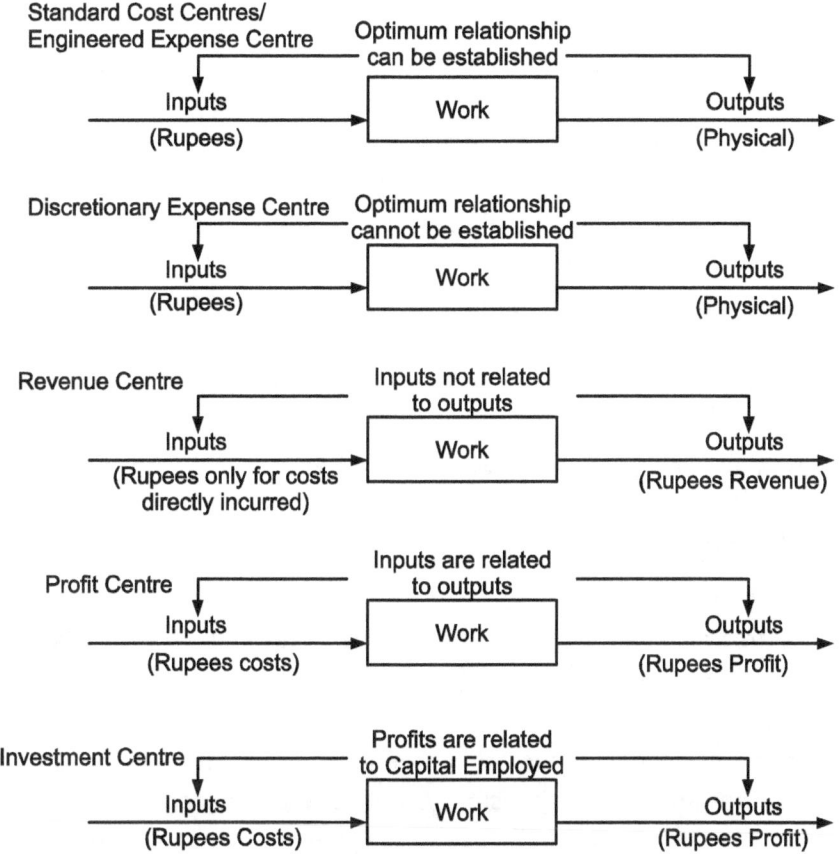

Fig. 5.4: Types of Responsibility Centres

5.2.5.1 Cost Centres

Cost centres generally produce goods or offer services to other parts of the firm. Because they only make goods or services, they have no control over sales prices and therefore can be assessed on the basis of their total costs.

One way for a cost centre to decrease costs is to purchase low-grade materials, but doing so damages the quality of finished goods. When dealing with cost centres, one must cautiously check the quality of goods.

A cost centre is a section of an organisation in which all costs are added, and the manager of this section is held accountable for the costs incurred though he is not responsible for revenue generation. In a manufacturing concern, the production and service departments are grouped as cost centres. The responsibility in a cost centre is limited to cost only. A cost centre is not held directly accountable for generating revenue in the organisation. Cost centre managers have a control over some or all of the costs that are collected at the cost centre. Thus, a cost centre is a level where the employees of that centre are just concerned with the cost management. A cost centre is also known as an expense centre. In this section of the responsibility centre, only the inputs are calculated in monetary terms and not the output as services provided by some departments of a cost centre are not calculable in monetary value. The performance of a cost centre is calculated in terms of quantity of inputs used for producing a specified output. The performance of the manager of a cost centre is assessed by comparing the costs incurred with the budgeted costs.

Expenses centres are of two types:

(a) Engineered costs: These are parts of cost for which the 'right' or 'proper' amount of costs can be approximated with a rational degree of dependability. The costs incurred in a factory for direct labour, material, components, supplies and utilities are examples.

(b) Discretionary costs or managed costs are those for which no such engineered approximation is possible; the amount of costs depend on management's judgement about the amount that is suitable under the conditions.

5.2.5.2 Revenue Centre

Revenue centres generally only have power over sales and have very less control over costs. To assess a revenue centre's performance, look only at its revenues and overlook everything else.

A manager of a revenue centre is held accountable for the revenue credited to the sub-unit. Revenue centres are those responsibility centres where managers are only accountable for financial outputs through generating sales revenue. A revenue centre's manager is also held responsible for selling expenses such as sales persons' salaries, commissions, and order receiving costs.

Revenue centres have some disadvantages. Their assessments are based completely on sales, so revenue centres have no motive to control costs. This kind of free rein motivates the entire concession managers to employ extra employees or to find other expensive ways to increase sales.

5.2.5.3 Profit Centres

Profits are the excess of revenue over the total costs. Therefore, the manager of a profit centre is held responsible for the revenues, costs, and profits of the centre. A profit centre is a responsibility centre in which inputs are calculated in terms of expenses and outputs are calculated in terms of revenues.

Profit centres are businesses within a big business, such as the individual stores that form a mall, whose managers take pleasure in controlling their own revenues and expenses. They frequently choose the merchandise to buy and sell, and they have the authority to put their own prices.

Profit centres are assessed on the basis of controllable margin, the difference between controllable revenues and controllable costs. Leave out all the non-controllable costs, such as allocated overheads or other indirect fixed costs, from the assessment. A good thing about running a profit centre is that it gives managers an incentive to do precisely what the firm desires, earn profits.

Categorising responsibility centres as profit centres has its own drawbacks. Although they get assessed on the basis of revenues and expenses, no one pays attention to their use of assets. This situation gives managers an inducement to use excessive assets to increase profits.

For managers, the advantage of using more assets is the increase in sales and profits. What's the drawback? There are no drawbacks of using assets; managers of profit centres are not held responsible for the assets that they use.

This fault in the assessment of profit centres can be tackled by carefully checking how profit centres use assets or by just reclassifying a profit centre as an investment centre.

Advantages of Profit Centres

(i)   It gives a powerful tool for measuring how well the profit centre has performed.

(ii) The profit centre looks like a business in miniature form and like a separate company, its profits are calculated. The managers are encouraged to take decisions about inputs and outputs in such a way, that profit of a profit centre is maximised. The profit centre acts as a good training ground for general management responsibility.

(iii) The profit centre makes decentralised organisation possible. Top management can securely hand over the power to the divisional managers because the profit centre reports give sufficient information about the successful performance of the operating managers. It gives a better and wider measurement of performance than the expense centres. If the managers are accountable for both revenue and expense aspects of performance, the contribution of each manager to the goal of the whole organisation is simple to measure than when no single manager is accountable for both revenues and expenses.

Illustration of Profit Centre Evaluation

ABC Ltd. uses a budgetary control system which measures performance based on its product divisions A and B. The budgeted and actual sales for a specific month are as follows

Division	Sales Quantity (₹) Budget	Sales Quantity (₹) Actual	Sales Revenue (₹) Budget	Sales Revenue (₹) Actual
A	40,000	48,000	4,00,000	4,80,000
B	80,000	80,000	4,00,000	4,80,000

The standard unit controllable variable costs are ₹ 4 and ₹ 2 for A and B respectively. The budgeted controllable fixed costs for the month are ₹ 40,000 each for products A and B. The attributable section costs budgeted are ₹ 80,000 and ₹ 1,20,000 for products A and B.

Presume these are no opening and closing inventories, the actual variable costs for the month were ₹ 1,68,000 and ₹ 1,92,000 for division A and b respectively. The actual controllable fixed costs amounted to ₹ 44,000 for division A and ₹ 52,000 for division B actual attributable segment costs ₹ 88,000 for A and ₹ 1,28,000 for B. The common company-wide costs are presumed to be ₹ 96,000 to be allocated based on the segment sales revenue.

Prepare a performance assessment report if ABC Ltd. uses a profit centre on the basis of divisional performance.

Solution: **Performance evaluation for the month (000)**

	Product Line A			Product Line B			Total		
	Budget	Actual	Variance	Budget	Actual	Variance	Budget	Actual	Variance
	₹	₹	₹	₹	₹	₹	₹	₹	₹
Sales revenue	400	480	80 F	400	480	80 F	800	960	160 F
less controllable variable costs	160	168	8 A	160	192	32 A	320	360	40 A
Controllable contribution margins	240	312	72 F	240	288	48 F	480	600	120 F
less controllable fixed costs	40	44	4 A	40	52	12 A	80	96	16 A
Controllable segment margin	200	268	68 F	200	236	36 F	400	504	104 F
less attributable segment costs	80	88	8 A	120	128	8 A	200	216	16 A
Segment profit contribution	120	180	60 F	80	108	28 F	200	288	88 F
less common firm wide costs	48	48	—	48	48	—	96	96	—
Net income	72	132	60 F	32	60	28 F	104	192	88 F

F = Favourable, A = Adverse

Note: Common firm-wide costs allocated based on budgeted sales revenue.

5.2.5.4 Investment Centres

It is defined as a responsibility centre in which inputs are measured in terms of cost/expenses and outputs are measured in terms of revenues and in which assets used are also measured. In other words, investment centres not only take costs and revenues into consideration but also the assets used in the division. As a responsibility centre, the performance of a unit would be measured in comparison to the revenues/profits and the assets used in a division. The importance of investment centre analysis is the connection between the profits and the assets that are used to generate those profits. It is thus an addition of the profit centre, as it covers all the parts that are related to the measurement of the overall performance of the company's different divisions. On the other hand, the investment centre is one step above a profit centre, in terms of the additional financial data.

The investment centre analysis can be used as a base for assessing the contribution of an entity and also the performance of a divisional manager. The measure of performance in an investment centre is founded on the relationship between the profits/income and the assets used in generating the profits. There are two ways to relate income to assets.

(a) Return on Investment (ROI) analysis: The return on investment is defined simply as the ratio of profit to investment.

$$ROI = \frac{\text{Profit after tax + Interest (1 – Tax)}}{\text{Investment}}$$

For example, if profit is ₹ 60,000 and investment is ₹ 400,000, the rate of return on investment is 60000/400,000 = 15 percent.

(b) Residual Income (RI) analysis or Economic Value Added (EVA): Economic value added (EVA) is the amount in rupees that remains after subtracting an "implied" interest charge from the functional income. The interest that is implied reflects an opportunity cost, and is charged on the amount of assets in each investment centre. The rate of interest charge is equivalent to the minimum rate on investment stated by top management as part of the corporate strategic plan. For example, a division has a budgeted income of ₹ 10 lakhs and a budgeted investment of ₹ 60 lakhs. The average cost of capital for the company is 12 percent. The budgeted residual income is:

Divisional income	₹ 10 lakhs
Interest charge	
12% on ₹ 60 lakhs	7.20
Residual income/	2.80
Economic value added	

Different interest rates may be applied to different components of investment like fixed assets, inventories, receivables and cash.

5.3 Management Control Systems of Service Organisations

5.3.1 Introduction

A management control system of service organisations generally explains the features that differentiate it from manufacturing organisations. It assists us in knowing the distinctive features of non-profit establishments as compared to profit-seeking organisations while designing control systems. It also assists us in knowing the issues involved in drafting management control systems in non-profit organisations.

5.3.2 Service Organisations in General

Service organisations and their management control systems are in general different from systems in manufacturing organisations. The features that make them different are –

1. **Absence of Inventory Buffer**

   Goods in a manufacturing organisation held in inventory are a buffer that diminishes the effect on production activity of variations in sales volume. Services cannot be stored, for example, airplane seat, hotel room, hospital operating room or the hours of lawyers, physicians, scientists and other professionals.

   The cost of many service organisations are basically fixed in the short-run. In brief, a hotel cannot decrease its costs considerably by blocking some of its rooms. In the same way, professional organisations like accounting and law companies hesitate to lay-off professionals at times of low sales volume due to its effect on self-esteem and costs of re-employing and training.

   An important variable in most service organisations is the degree to which present capacity is matched with the demand. This can be done in two ways. Firstly, to trigger demand in off-peak period is by marketing efforts and price concessions. Secondly, service organisations regulate the size of the personnel to expected demands by such measures as scheduling training activities in slack periods and compensating for long hours in busy periods.

2. **Difficulties in Controlling Quality**

   A manufacturing firm can check the products before they are shipped to the customer. A service firm cannot judge the quality of the product until the time the service is provided and then the judgements are often biased.

3. **Labour Intensive**

   Most service firms are labour intensive and cannot use tools and mechanise production lines by substituting labour and decreasing the costs. Hospitals do add costly tools but mostly to give better treatment and this increases cost.

4. **Multi-unit Organisations**

   Some service organisations operate many units in different locations with comparatively small units, for example, fast food restaurant chains, auto rented firms, gasoline service stations etc. Some of the units are owned, others operate under a franchise. The likeness of the separate units gives a common base for analysing budgets and assessing performance not available to the manufacturing firm.

5. **Historical Development**

   Cost accounting began in manufacturing firms to appreciate the work that is happening and finished goods inventories for financial statements. These systems provided information for use in setting selling prices and for other management purposes.

   Several service organisations are not required to develop cost data. Their use of product cost and other management accounting data is quite new.

5.3.3 Professional Service Organisations

Research and development organisations, law and accounting companies, health care organisations, engineering companies, architectural companies, consulting companies, advertising agencies etc. are examples of organisations whose products are professional services.

Special Characteristics

1. **Goals:** A professional organisation has comparatively a small number of tangible assets; its main asset is the skill of its professional employees which doesn't show in its balance sheet. Return on assets used, thus, is not related in such organisations. Their financial goal is to give sufficient compensation to the professionals.

   In several organisations, a related goal is to increase their size. It reflects economies of scale in using the efforts of central staff and units accountable for maintaining the organisations up-to-date.

2. **Professionals:** Professional organisations are labour intensive and the labour is of a special kind. Several professionals prefer to work alone rather than working as a team.

   Professionals have a tendency to give insufficient weightage to the financial implications of their decisions; they want to do the best job they can, despite its cost. This attitude has an effect on the attitude of support employees and non-professionals in the organisation, which causes an inadequacy in cost control.

3. **Output and Input Measurement:** The output of professional organisations cannot be calculated in physical terms, such as units, tonnes or gallons. We can determine the number of hours spent by a lawyer on a case but this is a measure of input not output. Output is the efficiency of the lawyer's work and this is not measured by the

number of pages or hours in the courtroom. The revenue earned is one measure of output in several professional organisations but these monetary amounts connect to the quantity of services provided, not to their quality. Moreover, the work that is completed by the professionals is non-repetitive. This makes it difficult to plan the time needed to achieve the task, to set reasonable standards to carry out a task and to judge how satisfying the performance was.

Some professionals particularly scientists, engineers and professors are unenthusiastic to keep a check of how they spend their time and this makes the task of measuring performance, difficult. However, complex problems arise in determining how time should be charged to customers, how to explain for the time spent, reading literature, going to meetings and otherwise keeping up-to-date?

4. **Small Size:** Professional organisations are comparatively small and work at a single place. The senior management can individually monitor which is going on and individually encourage employees. Thus, there is less need for a refined management control system with profit centres and formal performance reports.

5. **Marketing:** A clear separation between marketing activities and production activities does not exist in most organisations. In some cases professional ethical code restricts the amount and character of marketing efforts that is seen clearly by the experts. It is thus, hard to allot appropriate credit to the person accountable for "selling" a new customer.

Management Control Systems

1. **Pricing:** If the profession is one in which members are used to keeping a check on their time, fees usually are related to the professional time spent on the meeting. The hourly billing rate depends on the grade of the professional as well as a loading for overhead costs and profit. In other occupations such as investment banking, the fee is based on the monetary size of the security issue. In others, there is a price that is set for the assignment. Prices differ among professionals; they are comparatively low for research scientists and quite high for accountants and physicians.

2. **Profit Centres and Transfer Pricing:** Support units such as maintenance, information processing, transportation telecommunication, printing, and procurement of material and services, charge consuming units for their services. The principles for transfer pricing are similar to the relevant manufacturing firms.

3. **Strategy Planning and Budgeting:** The strategic plan of a professional organisation mainly includes a long-range recruitment plan rather than a developed plan for all aspects of the company's operation. The budgeting process in professional organisations is the same as the manufacturing organisations.

4. **Control of Operations:** The billed time ratio, which is the ratio of hours billed to total professional hours available, is watched closely.

   The incapability to set standards for task performance, the desirability of performing work by teams, the resulting problems of supervising a matrix organisation and the behavioural features of professionals make the planning and control of the daily functions in a professional organisation difficult. When the work is completed by project teams, control is focussed on the project. A written plan for each project is required, and timely reports should be ready that evaluate the original performance with planned performance in terms of cost, schedule and quality as done in management control of projects.

5. **Performance Measurement and Appraisal:** Appraisal of the big percentage of experts who are within the extremes is much more complex. For some occupations, for instance, the suggestions of an investment analyst can be compared with the original market behaviour of the securities, doctors skill level can be measured by the success ratio of operations.

These measures depend on suitable qualifications and in most situations the evaluation of performance is ultimately a matter of human judgement by superiors, peers, self, subordinates and customers.

Judgements made by superiors are the most common. Professional organisations are more and more using formal systems to gather performance appraisals and talk about the employees and discuss matters with the expert. Some systems need numerical ratings of specified traits of performance and provide for weighted average of these ratings. Compensation may be fixed partly to these numerical ratings. In a matrix organisation, both the project leader and the head of the functional unit judge the performance.

Appraisal by professional peers, or by subordinates, is occasionally a part of a formal control system. In a number of organisations, people are asked to make a self-appraisal.

The budget can be used as a basis for measuring cost performance and the original time taken can be compared with the planned time. Budgeting and control of discretionary expenses are as significant in a professional company as in a manufacturing firm. Such financial measures are comparatively insignificant in evaluating a professional's contribution to the company's profitability. The professional's major contribution is related to quantity and above all the quality of work and appraisal is mostly biased.

In some occupations, internal audit processes are used to control quality.

5.3.4 Financial Service Organisations

Financial service organisations include commercial bank and thrift institutions, insurance and security companies. These firms are in business mainly to manage money.

General Observations

The financial services sector comprises a significant backbone to world economies.

Before some years, commercial banking, investment banking, retail brokerage and insurance continued as separate industries; companies specialised in a single industry and tended to compete in a single country. Deregulation has removed industry and geographic boundaries.

Financial services companies have used the information technology revolution to invent new products and find out new techniques of trading.

The need for controls in the financial services sector has become vital, for instance, Asian financial crises during the second half of 1990s, was partly the result of inadequate controls in banks in Thailand, Indonesia, Japan and other Asian countries.

During the 1990s new companies of financial instruments designed by financial service companies occasionally resulted in huge losses for the customers.

Ultimately, the corporate scandals during 2002 created a big push for investment banks to spin off their research departments.

Special Characteristics

While the general principles and concepts of management control systems apply, they are required to be adjusted to the following special characteristics of financial services industry.

(a) **Monetary Assets:** Most of the assets of financial companies are monetary. The present value of monetary assets is more easily calculated than the value of place and other physical assets or patents and other intangible assets. When dollars held by all firms have a similar value, estimated at both its face amount and its purchasing power. Financial assets can be transferred from one owner to another easily and quickly.

(b) **Time Period of Transactions:** The performance of those engaged in bond issue, a mortgage loan or in selling and pricing the insurance policy cannot be calculated at the time the important decision is made. Control requires that there is a way of continuously observing the transaction during its life, including periodic audits of all outstanding loans.

Some transactions are finished fast based on the information that is acquired instantly or over a period. Thus, there is a need for a system to report securities and to evaluate the risk to the organisation if prices move against the traders' securities.

(c) **Risk and Reward:** Most business decisions involve a trade-off between risk and reward. The bigger the risk, the bigger should be the anticipated reward. In financial services companies, this trade-off is more clear than in business investment such as involved in purchase of a machine or the launching of a new product.

(d) Technology: Technology has revolutionised the financial service industry. Financial service companies have used information technology as a way to provide innovative services.

5.3.5 Health Care Organisations

Health care organisations include hospitals, clinics and similar physicians, organisations, health maintenance organisations, retirement and nursing homes, home care organisations, and medical laboratories, among others.

Special Characteristics

1. **Different social problem:** The current health care delivery system is impracticable. However, the cost per treatment is rising with the development of new equipment and new drugs. Conversely, the number of ill persons is increasing.

2. **Change in mix of providers:** Within the overall increase in health care cost, important changes have happened in the way in which health care is delivered and, thus, in the practicability of particular types of providers. Many services that were conventionally given in hospitals on an inpatient basis are not given in clinics or in patients' homes. Businessmen have entered the industry to give these new services.

3. **Third party payers:** About more than 3/4th of the health care is given by government and insurance companies, and the balance by individual patients.

    Due to an increase in hospitals costs per patient and businessmen entering the field, a need has been felt to set up sophisticated cost accounting systems; generally the systems are bought from an outside software organisation and then adjusted to one's requirements. These systems give information on individual patients and they give a report of the real costs in comparison with the standard costs for each diagnostic related shop on which insurance firm and other service providers compensate costs; costs are categorised by departments and by attending physicians within departments.

    This information is besides the information conventionally collected in hospitals; it concentrates on outputs plus inputs.

4. **Professionals:** The management control implications of professionals are same as those talked about earlier. Their main loyalty is to the occupation rather than to the organisations. Department managers are professionals whose management function is only part-time; the chief of surgery does surgery. In the past, physicians have tended to give little emphasis to cost control.

5. **Importance of Quality Control:** The health care industry deals with human lives, so the quality of the service it provides is of supreme importance.

Management Control Process

Subject to the features that are explained above, the management control process in the health care industry is the same as the manufacturing organisation. Due to the change in the product mix and due to a rise in the quantity and cost of new equipment, the strategic planning process in hospitals is significant. The preparation of the annual budget is conservative. Vast quantities of data are quickly available for the control of operating activities. Financial performance is analysed by comparing the original revenues and expenses with budgets, recognising significant variances and taking suitable actions on them.

5.3.6 Government Organisations

Government organisations are service organisations and except for business like activities, they are non-profit organisations. Thus, the features that are explained above, apply to these organisations. Their business like activities such as electricity and water utilities function like their private sector counterparts.

Special Characteristics

(i)   **Political influences:** In government organisations, decisions result from numerous and frequently from conflicting pressures. The elected officials that are to be re-elected promote the perceived requirements of their constancy although they may not be in the best interests of society altogether. These differing pressures result in less than best decisions. The managers may be prohibited from making sound business decisions; they may be needed to support particular suppliers or to employ political supporters. Strict procurement policies and civil service regulations have reduced these pressures to some level.

(ii) **Public information:** In a democratic society the press and public think that they have a right to know everything about a government organisation, due to the laws of freedom of information. Some media stories exaggerate too much about mismanagement. Thus, to decrease opportunities for media gossip stories, government managers have taken some steps to restrict the amount of sensitive, controversial information that flows through the formal management control system. This diminishes the efficiency of the system.

(iii) **Attitude towards clients:** Profit firms and many non-profit organisations, acquire their revenues from clients, thus these organisations welcome the actual and potential clients and befriend them. Most government organisations are supported by the public; they get their revenues from the general public. Extra clients are a load for them, because they create further demand on the service ability, generating poor services and the rude attitude of the bureaucrats. Managers recognise this and do their best to convince employees to offer good service.

(iv) **Red tape:** The government has propagated huge number of rules and regulations. Some of these are required; others are responses to small errors that become highly publicised.

(v) **Management compensation:** Managers and other professionals in government organisations are likely to be less compensated than their counterparts in business. As a result, the best managers do not go into public service. There are exceptions to specific types of scientists and engineers. Therefore, there is a problem of rewarding good performance.

(vi) **Financial accounting:** Accounting standards for state and local government are set by the government accounting standards.

Management Control Systems

1. **Strategic Planning and Budget Preparation:** Strategic planning is significant in government organisations. The managers and legislations must make hard decisions about the allotment of resources. Some of these decisions reflect political stress, others are the caused because of sophisticated analysis, particularly benefit/cost methods which are becoming more and more formalised. The annual budget process is also a significant control device in government as it is in other non-profit organisations.

2. **Performance measurement:** Expenses can be calculated precisely in government organisations as in business. Revenue is not a measure of output in government organisations. Government has developed non-monetary pointers, which can be categorised as (i) results measures, (ii) process measures and (iii) social indicators.

A results measure also called as outcomes measure is a measure of output that is connected to the organisation's goals. As for example, number of students graduating, number of kilometres of roads finished. These measures do not give correct measure of the output; the number of graduates shows nothing about how well the students were learned.

A process measure is connected to an activity performed by the organisation. For example, the number of livestock examined in a week, number of purchase orders issued in a day or number of lines entered in the computer in an hour. These measures are simple to translate as there is a close causal connection between the inputs and the process measure. Efficiency can be determined and not the effectiveness, that is, how far it has accomplished the organisation's goals.

A social pointer is a broad measure of output that reflects the effect of the work of the organisation. As social pointers are affected by outer forces they are at best a sign of achievements of the organisation itself. For instance, life expectancy is a sign of the effectiveness of the country's health care system but it is also affected by standard of living, dietary and smoking habits and other causes. Social pointers are helpful in analysing long-range strategic problems.

5.3.7 Management Control in Banking Sector

General Characteristics: Commercial banks earn income mainly by giving a loan and investing money. The interest on this money is their revenue. They get the money mainly by attracting deposits. The interest they pay on these deposits corresponds more or less to cost of sales in a manufacturing firm. Thus net interest expense, income, which is the difference between interest revenue and interest, is an important number for bank management to observe it corresponds to gross margin in a manufacturing firm. If the difference between the interest revenue and interest expense as well as revenue from other activities, more than covers its operating costs and loan losses, the bank is profitable. Commercial banks are regulated by the Central Bank Authority.

Management Control Implications

1. **Interest rates:** The relationship between interest revenue and interest expense is an important variable. Banks frequently calculate the amount of interest-sensitive assets, interest-sensitive liabilities and the 'gap' which is the difference between them, is the bank's interest rate exposure; both prudent management and rules of regulatory bodies require that it be kept within specific limits.

    Banks refer to the elements of risk as 'Four Cs' – the borrower's general character, its ability to pay back the loan from wages or other sources, its capital on net assets, and the collateral promised for the particular loan. For accepting bigger risks, the bank expects a bigger reward. Senior management has the job of setting the rates on loans of different risks and maturities, of setting equivalent ratio for deposits and of guaranteeing that the actions of the individual managers amount to a satisfactory interest rate for the bank in total. The management control system must guarantee that its rates correspond all through the organisation and that they are followed.

    Volume: Most expenses are fixed in the short-term. Therefore, if a bank can raise its volume of deposits, other things being equal, it will be capable of making more loans and the increased gross margin will increase its profits.

2. **Loan losses:** The central bank including the government has inflicted strict restrictions for "non-performing loans" (that is, loans whose payments, are delinquent). These stop the bank from making additional loans.

3. **Expenses:** Most of the expenses in a bank are personnel related and are subject to budgeting and controls that are similar to the controls in a manufacturing company.

4. **Other income:** Banks earn income by managing trust accounts, collecting receivables and carrying out different other services for customers. Such services should be provided a cost as well as a profit margin.

5. **Joint revenues:** A depositor whose account is maintained in one branch can do business at another branch. Branch managers want to get credit for the revenues that

they produce by such activities and to be compensated for services that they provide to customers of other branches. If the bank is prearranged into profit centres, the allocation of joint revenues can have an important effect on profits.

6. **Profit centres:** Several commercial banks establish profit centres, for their branches or for their individual headquarters activities or both. In that case, the transfer price for money should be solved. This price is an expense to activities that make loans and investments and it is revenue to activities that generate deposits. Some branches are 'loan heavy' (that is, their loans exceed their deposits) and others are 'deposit heavy'; profitability will not be calculated properly unless the transfer price is reasonable to each kind. If the transfer price for the cost of money is set too low, the profitability of the loan-heavy branches will be exaggerated, but if it is set too high, the profitability of deposit heavy branches will be exaggerated.

Measurement of cost of money is also significant in measuring the profitability of loans with different maturities, loans with different risk features and loans to different markets.

Expense centres: Since transfer price is very controversial, some banks decided not to develop transfer prices; there they control branches as expense centres. In such circumstances, they measure performance by such pointers as unit or rupees output per staff member, rupees of revenue and market share by product type, expenses for rupees of revenue compared with budget and quality pointers. Some use a management by objectives (MBO) system, in which the main objective is to get a certain number of extra customers. They make special analysis of profitability as a basis for establishing prices and for making decisions about opening and closing branches and adding or stopping the services.

In comparing the performance of many branches, measuring the volume is a problem. The total of each type of transactions can be completed but computing these individual totals into an overall measure of volume can be misleading, unless differences in the effort needed for the different types are considered.

5.3.8 Management Control in the Insurance Sector

Insurance firms also deal with money. They collect money in the form of premiums, invest it, and later expend money in the form of claims, death benefits, or annuities. Many years might pass between the time a policy is written and the time when benefit payments are done. The profitability of the policy cannot be understood with certainty until the last payment is made, but for the reasons of management control the firm cannot wait; it presently requires information.

Conventionally, insurance firms measured the performance of their responsibility centres by an accurate guide, such as the amount of first year premiums or the face amount of insurance written. Recently, they have started exploring the possibility of measuring the profitability of a policy while it is being written. For instance, the annual premium on a normal life policy is reached by considering life expectancy, approximate investment income, selling costs, and recurring operating costs over the life of the policy, regulated if required to meet rates charged by other firms. Each of these parts is set conventionally, for instance, the mortality table used in setting premiums minimises the actual life expectancy. The final profitability of the policy occurs from the difference between these traditional estimates and the actual amounts experienced. The true expectations can be estimated, and from them the expected present value of the policy can be decided. Therefore, a measure of profitability can be calculated at the time the policy is sold.

With this measure of profitability as an initial point, insurance firms can organise their sales branches as profit centres, and they can also measure the performance of the investment, actuarial, and other parts, of the firm by comparing the original results with those used in the calculations of the current value of a policy's profitability.

Life Insurance

- Offers economic support for survivors such as dependents and existing spouses.
- Provides liquidity to satisfy estate tax and other estate obligations.
- Allows companies to counterbalance the economic loss caused by the death of an employee.
- Allows you to collect funds for retirement, emergencies, and other needs usually on a tax-advantaged basis.
- Life insurance needs differ depending on the family's life cycle.
- There are usually three stages of the family life cycle: Family years, middle years, and retirement years.

During the family years, the need for insurance increases radically throughout the early years of a family who have people depending on them. It remains high until either the customer's investment income rises or the needs of his or her dependents reduce. As the dependent's requirements change often, coverage should be re-examined regularly and adjusted in accordance with the requirements at different stages of their lives.

There are two major types of life insurance: term and cash value. Term coverage is death protection for a particular period of time paying benefits only if the insured dies before the term policy expires. Cash value life insurance allows cash to rise after a while as the premium includes two components, a pure insurance protection and a savings aspect.

The two types of cash value life insurance are whole life and variable life policies.

	Advantages	**Disadvantages**
Term Life Insurance	Low cost	No component of savings
	Flexible, allowing change in level of coverage to match needs	
Cash Value Insurance	Build up of cash savings	Costs more than term life over the life of policy
		Limited investment options

In addition of having the correct type and amount of life insurance coverage, it is significant to have the policy-holder name their beneficiaries at the time they buy the policy. Contingent beneficiaries should also be named in the event that the main beneficiaries die before the insured. If no beneficiary is named, the insurance proceeds and the rest of the policyholder's estate will go through the process of probate, which is frequently both time-consuming and costly. The owner of the policy can change beneficiaries whenever he or she wishes to. Each time a major change happens, such as an addition to the family, divorce, death, or change in residence, the policy owner should reassess his or her choice of beneficiaries. Careful thought should be given as to the owner of a life insurance policy as part of the estate planning process.

5.4 Management Control System in a Non-Profit Organisation

5.4.1 Non-Profit Organisations

The word "non-profit" tends to have negative implications because it tells us what these organisations do, not what they do.

A non-profit organisation is one that is chartered to work in the interests of the society. It operates free of any obligation to pay income-taxes. It is limited by definition from taking part in equity markets as it has no shareholders. Its sources of funds are obtained from contributions, grants, operating surplus and debts instruments of different kinds. The main goal of non-profits is defined by their mission.

Non-profit institutions may be classified into two groups – Government organisations and private tax-exempt organisations. Private organisations can be further divided into commercial organisation and charitable groups; the former consists of trade unions, trade associations and clubs and the latter consists of hospitals, religious groups, research, educational and social service organisations.

5.4.2 Profit-Oriented Corporations vs. Non-Profit Organisations

A profit-oriented corporation is an organisation whose survival depends on selling its products or services to potential customers of its products at a profit. A non-profit organisation is an organisation whose goal is to give services for the good of the community and/or on humanitarian grounds, without getting any financial compensation in return.

Covering the non-profit sector, the main interest in this paper is placed on charitable social service organisations. These organisations are required to greatly depend on public support given by governments and foundations. This means that their revenues do not openly measure the value of services given to the beneficiaries. Generally in this type of organisation, those that give support have a tendency to use a lot of influence over the activities of the organisation. Certain United Nations agencies like the Red Cross and Save the Children can be cited as examples.

5.4.3 Distinctive Characteristics of Non-Profit Organisations

Designing control systems for non-profit institutions is different from profit-seeking institutions. The principal features of these institutions that cause variations in their control systems are:

1. **The absence of a profit measure:** Performance evaluation is more difficult.

2. **Different tax and legal status:** These institutions are not taxed and no shareholders exist.

3. **The tendency of non-profit organisations to be service organisations**. This makes the measurement of the quantity and quality of service provided very difficult.

4. **Greater constraints on goals and strategies:** Donors may limit the use of funds to prearranged purposes.

5. **Less dependence on customers for financial support:** Several people rely on endowed sources of support thus making them less reliant upon situations for support.

6. **The dominance of professionals:** Functional pressures on the goals of an organisation can be formed, as these employees have dual commitments, to the organisation and to their occupation.

7. **Differences in senior management:** Frequently these organisations are run by professionals trained in another field besides management such as college professors, musical artists, ministers and priests and doctors.

8. **A tradition of inadequate management controls:** This too is derived from a tendency in these organisations for management to be made up of professionals who value professional goals but who underestimate management skills.

5.4.4 Issues Involved in Drafting Management Control System in a Non-Profit Organisation

The issues involved in drafting management control system in a non-profit organisation can be discussed in the following heads –

1. The mission of non-profits
2. Stakeholders goals
3. Key success factors
4. Performance measures
5. Infra structure
6. Management style and culture
7. Formal control process
8. Communication systems
9. Rewards
10. Informal control process

1. **Mission of Non-profit:** Non-profits are organised so as to follow and achieve a mission, that is, its purpose. Drucker stresses that a mission statement should contain the following three parts –

   (a) The opportunities that the organisation can exploit or requirements that it can meet.

   (b) The strengths of the organisation.

   (c) What members of the organisation believe in.

2. **Stakeholder's goal:** In a non-profit organisation, there frequently is no principal stakeholder but a multiplicity of major stakeholders; for instance a school board, a church or a child care agency has numerous important stakeholders.

   Boards or Trustees are the major stakeholders because they are the major donors and contributions of time and effort. The board represents a real opportunity for these institutions so long as they concentrate on attaining the mission of the establishment and stay out of functioning details. The purpose of the board is to direct the mission of the institution by assessing important strategies, to choose the CEO, to provide and secure funds, to offer professional viewpoint on governance and to make the CEO responsible for the achievement of the mission.

   Besides the brand, each non-profit organisation has mission stakeholders to serve, to save the lost, to heal the sick, to protect abused children, to educate children and so on. Besides, there are external parties who do not take part directly in the affairs of the establishment that have an important interest in the establishment, such as the public in the work of a school district.

Several employees and volunteers in a non-profit organisation take part because they believe in the mission of the organisation. But they believe in different parts of the organisation; for instance, physicians regard hospitals as a place to provide service to the patients and they want beds and other services to be available for the patients, irrespective of the cost. They are not worried about hospital money and they oppose contractual arrangements that get in the way with their practices and consequently there is frequently a disagreement between hospital administrators and the physicians employed at the hospital.

In formulating the stakeholders' goals it is necessary to put together all of the stakeholders goals around the missions of the organisation.

3. **Key success factors:** Key success factors for many non-profit establishments are the number of volunteers that it is capable of attracting and the number of volunteers it is capable of training at different level of quality.

Another important variable is fund development, as nearly everyone depends on the support of the people, particularly the volunteers, for contributions to support its paid staff and its programme.

Another important variable is the capability to attract the quantity and quality of board member it requires.

4. **Performance measures:** Performance measures should be set for each important success factor for each goal. Reports on these performance measures should be made and distributed to those accountable for their management.

We should try to quantify as many measurements as possible. Some are relatively simple to quantify. Others are not so simple to measure but are all the same important. But even these important variables that are not easily quantified may have quantitative replacements.

5. **Infrastructure:** Non-profits have a tendency to flatter organisational structure. Organisations tend to be functional and the functions are lead by professionals for instance, doctors, social workers, ministers, professors. Typical responsibility centres in a child care agency are social work, operations, administration and education. They tend to be cost centres unless revenue is generated, in which case they are either revenue centres or contribution centres.

The modern hospital has a dual organisation structure, one for the medical side of the establishment, and the other for administrative services. The medical side is controlled by physicians and a wide variety of technical and support staff. The administrative services consist of housekeeping, food service, maintenance, billing and accounting. A good deal of independence is generally granted to the hospital departments lead by professionals such as nursing, laboratory, pathology, radiology, surgery and so on. Most of these departments are cost centres, where quality of care and generally cost performance is the important performance measures. Several hospitals have created SBUs for recognisable sections of the hospital such as outpatient surgery, obstetrics, pharmacy, emergency room, physical medicine etc. which are profit centres and are set up for strategic planning and implementation purposes.

6. **Management style and culture:** The small and mid-sized ones are likely to assume the personality traits of the executive director and if he is a professional there is an inclination to place main attention upon his area of interest or training and has little feelings for the management.

In case of a hospital, dual structure causes an adversarial but co-dependent style. To manage the establishment successfully, control must be maintained on the medical side of the organisation. A general theme that seems to be persistent in all departments of the hospitals is that they are delivering health care of the highest quality possible.

7. **Formal control process:** The formal control tool is the budget. The budgeting process is difficult in the nonexistence of clear, scientific performance objectives for assessing programmes. As a part of programme assessment, it is necessary to decide the programme costs. Programme costs are generally subdivided into two groups: direct and indirect. In most non-profits, overhead is allocated on the basis of direct labour costs.

In case of a hospital, control within the medical side is required for quality patient care. This is done by using the patient record chart, which is separated into several sections containing progress notes, reports, and requests for all diagnostic and therapeutic procedures carried out within each department, there are several levels of control that is connected to the patient care mission to guarantee the highest-quality care.

A hospital is divided into different mission centres, that is, departments that work with patients directly, for example, in-patient care, and laboratory radiology. Service centres such as housekeeping, laundry and medical records provide support to each of the mission centres. Also, there are other support costs such as supplies, depreciation and insurance that serve as both service and mission centres. Programme costing then involves selecting the final cost objective such as cost of care per day or cost linked with a specific diagnostic group. To do this, all direct costs that are linked with the final costs objective are traced to that cost objective. To assign indirect costs, the standard practice is to take cost of support pools and allot them to both service and mission centres on the basis of allocation criteria that had the closest bearing on how the costs were incurred. The service centre cost is allotted to mission centres using the allocation base that mostly reflect the demand for service activities in mission centres. Cost variances as compared to budget can be worked out and analysed.

8. **Communication systems:** Board members, if organised correctly, can give a very important contribution to the communication systems of the non-profit institutions. If their strategic work is organised by the committee and each committee meets frequently with the related operating committee to add vision and its point of view, the board can play a very strong function in furthering the mission of the organisation.

   In case of hospitals, there is plethora of communication mechanisms within both the medical and administrative sides. On the medical side, there is generally a computerised hospital information system that gives updated patient information at nursing stations and contributes to the patient control process. The medical committees include physicians trying to work out the best course of treatment for a specific patient. These committees start to change physician behaviour to attain better cost performance while giving the highest quality of care.

9. **Rewards:** The paid staff plus the volunteer staff is dedicated to the mission of the organisation, therefore financial rewards are not very significant. Promotion opportunities are also not common.

   In case of hospitals, the main rewards are derived when one is happy after fulfilling the mission of giving high-quality health care. Physicians are paid well but other professionals are paid a little lesser than their counterparts in the profit sector. There are hardly any promotions in hospitals, given the flat organisation structure. There is little crossover from the medical side to the administrative side.

10. **Informal Control Process:** Interpersonal relationship: Because of fewer measurements, informal communication, networking and politics are likely to be the important processes for making resource allocation decisions.

   Informal control process: Medical managements of patients have a tendency to be very flexible to the progression and resolution of diseases. Management flexibility, however, has in history been much less demonstrable.

   Informal rewards: The strong culture of concern and pride in patient care is rewarded with a sense of achievement, providing strong information rewards. Many positions give a reasonable degree of status within a hospital. Surely, the physicians and administrators are in positions of high status.

   Informal communications: Informal communication tends to be very common and natural among peers but more limited between departments.

Points to Remember

- The sequence in which the control process takes place has been identified as follows.
  1. Strategic planning
  2. Budget preparation.
  3. Management control of operations
  4. Analysing performance reports and evaluating managerial performance
  5. Management compensation as it relates to management control process
- **Reward systems** are a main motivational tool to protect the participation of people to attain organisational goals.
- The **balanced scorecard** is designed to be a strategic management tool that allows organisations to interpret strategic goals into related measures of performance.
- **Benchmarking** is a constant process of comparing products and operations with the strongest competitors or the best practices in related operations of the best performing firm.
- A **responsibility centre** uses inputs, such as physical quantities of material, hours of different kinds of labour and variety of services.
- A **cost centre** is a section of an organisation in which all costs are added, and the manager of this section is held accountable for the costs incurred though he is not responsible for revenue generation.
- **Revenue centres** generally only have power over sales and have very less control over costs.
- **Profit centres** are businesses within a big business, such as the individual stores that form a mall, whose managers take pleasure in controlling their own revenues and expenses.
- **Investment Centres** is defined as a responsibility centre in which inputs are measured in terms of cost/expenses and outputs are measured in terms of revenues and in which assets used are also measured.
- A **non-profit organisation** is one that is chartered to work in the interests of the society.

Questions for Discussion

1. What are the contents of management control in small and medium enterprises?
2. Explain the methodology of implementing management control systems.
3. Discuss the tools and techniques for implementing management control systems.
4. What are the roles and responsibilities in implementing management control?
5. What is responsibility centres? Explain the types of responsibility centres.
6. Write a short note on
   (a) Cost Centres
   (b) Revenue Centres
   (c) Profit Centres
   (d) Investment Centres
7. Discuss the management control systems of service organisations.
8. Explain the management control system in a non-profit organisation.

■■■

(2013 Pattern)

Time : Three Hours   **Maximum Marks : 80**

N.B. : *All questions are compulsory and carry equal marks.*

1. Define Management Control. Explain the principles and types of Management Control.   **[15]**

OR

Define Marketing Control System. Explain tools and techniques of marketing control.   **[15]**

2. What is Project? Explain its aspects and factors affecting project.

OR

What is Project Planning? How do you plan the Cost Dimensions in the Project Management?   **[15]**

OR

3. What is Management Control Systems? Explain the commandments of effective control system.   **[15]**

OR

Define Production Control? Explain procedure and techniques of production control.   **[15]**

4. Define Inventory Control? Explain classification of Inventories.   **[15]**

OR

Explain Management Control System in Service and Non-Profit Organisatons.   **[15]**

5. Write short notes on (any four):   **[20]**
   (a) Kind of Control Devices
   (b) Control in Personnel Area
   (c) Stock Levels
   (d) Investment Centre
   (e) Computers and Information System
   (f) Decision Support System.

■■■

Notes

www.ingramcontent.com/pod-product-compliance
Lightning Source LLC
Chambersburg PA
CBHW080732020726
47503CB00010B/2889